WHEN DAYLIGHT BREAKS

AN AGENTS OF HIS NOVEL

SHEILA KELL

USA

When Daylight Breaks
Copyright @ 2025 by Sheila Kell
Cunningham Publishing

Editing and Formatting: Lea Schizas
Photographer: Paul Henry Serres
Photography
Model: Francis Hudon-Leblanc

ISBN (Print): 978-1-957587-19-6
ISBN (Digital): 978-1-957587-18-9

Printed in the USA

Titles by Sheila Kell

To Cindy S. Montgomery

I sincerely appreciate your providing the book title and your unwavering support. Your thoughtfulness means a great deal to me. Thank you for being such a great source of encouragement!

Chapter One

They say love stinks, but for Elena Raymundo, the real stench came from being out of love. After spending three long years with Mark Thompson, she finally confronted the painful truth that she had wasted her time on a relationship destined for stagnation. Deep down, she knew she would never say "I do" to someone she didn't truly love. Was it insecurity that had kept her tethered to this unfulfilling romance, or had there been something more profound at play?

"You can't do this!" Disbelief roughened Mark's voice as she placed the last box of her belongings in the living room. She had been foolish to move in with him without a backup plan. When an apartment in a secure building became available, she jumped on it—before she even admitted to herself she was going to leave Mark.

Now, she was desperate to avoid the messy confrontation she feared Mark was about to unleash.

"It's done."

Mark kicked the box, a sharp sound that echoed in the quiet room.

Elena's thoughts flared like a rapidly building wildfire. She would not allow him to bully her into staying in their dead-end relationship.

"Is this your way of punishing me for not backing your decision to leave SWAT for some mysterious organization?"

Among other things. It just took me three years to realize you're really an asshole. "No. Well—" she paused, reconsidering her words. "—maybe just a bit, but mostly I feel we're just wasting time together. The truth is, we're not in love, Mark."

He stepped closer, and a shiver ran through Elena. Although he had never harmed her, uncertainty flickered in her mind. She couldn't shake the fear that he might attempt to draw her into his embrace. "But I love you, Elena." His voice was thick with emotion. "I've loved you from the moment our paths crossed."

Elena released a heavy sigh, frustration evident in her exhale. The man stood there, utterly oblivious. "But you're not in love with me."

"What the hell are you talking about? I told you I love you." His voice sliced through the air, sharp and demanding, leaving Elena feeling a surge of unease.

"Mark, don't make this messy. Let me get my things and go."

He closed the distance between them, and she instinctively stepped back. "No."

Elena couldn't help but catch the hint of challenge in his tone.

"I know you love me."

She clung to him in a moment of vulnerability,

thinking her feelings were love. But now, with Tiki—her courageous and injured police dog—by her side, a new chapter was unfolding, and she realized she'd thought it was love out of fear of the loneliness that had loomed ahead of her.

Elena, a former K9 handler with Baltimore SWAT, had faced her fair share of disrespectful men who failed to recognize her worth. However, in this new chapter of her life—much like her bold decision to leave SWAT—she was ready to seize control and reshape her narrative, driven by the deep desire to find love and acceptance on her terms.

Elena swiftly maneuvered around the table, her heart pounding in anticipation as she reached for the door. She would return when he wasn't home to retrieve her belongings.

With a determined pull, she flung it open. "It's time for me to leave."

But he was faster. With a fierce stride, he stalked toward her, slamming the door with a resounding thud. "I'll decide when it's time for you to leave," he growled, angry eyes locking onto hers. "You aren't leaving me."

This definitely isn't going as expected.

"No one leaves me." He lunged forward, a feral resolve carved into his face, eyes bright with possession.

But this time, she was quicker. With a swift sidestep, she slipped into her defensive stance, her heart racing. Uncertainty loomed over her—what would Mark do next? Yet, she wouldn't stand idly by, unprepared for whatever came her way.

"Mark, the time has come for me to go. Our

relationship has reached its end. Can't you see that?" And your behavior has been increasingly rude to those around you—impatience and even hints of racism now cloud your judgment. I can't take it anymore. It was truly disheartening that she only realized this much too late.

Four years ago, she was thrilled to be selected for the SWAT team, feeling like she was on top of the world. But her excitement quickly faded as the men on the team began to harass her, shattering her dreams. Just when she thought all hope was lost, Mark—charming and wealthy —swept into her life like a fairytale prince. With stars dancing in her eyes, she clung to the idea that someone as extraordinary as he could truly love her. Yet despite her longing, the elusive spark that signifies being "in love" remained achingly absent, leaving her heart in turmoil.

He narrowed his eyes, hatred flickering within them. "All I see before me is a worthless half-Mexican girl who couldn't even protect her dog while on the SWAT team. So?" he sneered. "She quit."

That did it. She was going to kick his ass for that comment. At just five feet four inches tall in her combat boots, she could effortlessly defend herself and take down any threat. Right now, however, Mark was rapidly transforming into the very threat she faced daily.

"Mark, let's not make this nasty. Please, just let me get my things and leave."

He advanced toward her, but she stood her ground with fierce determination this time. When he reached for her arm, a surge of adrenaline coursed through her, prompting her to strike back violently—her foot connected with a swift kick to his groin. She was fully aware it was a low blow, but the hurtful, racist comment had pushed her past the breaking point.

Mark clutched himself, doubling over as a groan of pain escaped his lips. "You bitch."

Elena felt a surge of amusement bubble up, but she quickly stifled it, recognizing that this moment contained no humor. Realizing she'd never get out of there with Mark around, she pulled away and swiftly reached into her cargo pants pocket, wrapped her fingers around her phone, and pulled it free. She dialed a number—a trusted contact within the force, someone she knew would have her back.

"Luis, I need you up here."

"I'm already here. Be right there."

She had prepped Luis Rodriguez, her ally on the force, who eagerly supported her during this crucial transition. His presence gave her the reassurance she desperately needed.

Mark lay on the floor, his breaths gradually steadying, signaling his ability to rise. "You called the cops! I didn't even lay a finger on you. It was you who assaulted me."

Luis, clad in full police gear, his heavy utility belt clinking with each step, busted through the door and instantly took in the scene before him. His gaze landed on Mark, sprawled on the floor, a grin creeping across his face. "My, my, how the mighty have fallen." His Mexican-accented voice dripped with amusement and triumph.

Mark had always looked down on Luis, treating him as if he were beneath him. This condescending attitude extended to any of her friends, except for the stunning women who could easily walk the runway. It was as if only beauty—and money—could command his respect.

"Luis, Mark was just about to leave. Would you be a dear and escort him out?"

Mark rose to his feet. Hatred etched across his face as he stepped toward her.

But Luis was quicker, positioning himself between them just before Mark's foot hit the ground. "Let's just call it quits, shall we? It's time for you to go."

Fueled by anger, Mark jerked away, a storm brewing in his eyes. "I demand that she be arrested for assault!" He leveled an accusatory finger at Elena, his voice echoing with tension in the air.

Luis let out a frustrated sigh, shaking his head as he glanced towards Mark. "You know I'm not going to do that."

Mark's face twisted in disdain. "You're all the same, always banding together." He turned to Elena. With his voice laced with venom, he spat, "You'll regret this, Elena. I swear it."

"Is that a threat?" Luis questioned in a low but steady voice.

Mark glared back, his eyes narrowing. "That's not just a threat. That's a promise."

"Luis," Elena intervened, her tone urgent, "just let it go. Please, let him go."

Mark glanced at his watch and turned back to her. "You'll regret this." Then he stormed out of the house.

Elena released a breath of air and turned to Luis.

Before she could thank him, his gaze full of concern

captured hers. "Are you okay?"

She nodded. "Yes."

"All right. I'll keep an eye on him to ensure he doesn't cause any trouble for you."

"Thank you, Luis."

Gathering her last box and purse, they left the house, with Elena unable to deadbolt it because her keys were on the kitchen counter for Mark. Sighing, she trudged to the driveway with Luis beside her.

After Luis left, she turned to her running SUV, her heart pounding as she set the box on the back seat.

Had Mark truly been on the brink of hurting her? The unsettling thought sent shivers down her spine. Determined to protect herself, she resolved to remain vigilant until she was certain he had calmed down and found someone else to claim as his next trophy girlfriend.

With a jolt, Elena snapped back to reality, her pulse returning to normal as she approached the driver's side door. An eager whine echoed in the SUV. When she flung the door open, Tiki sprang forward, her spirited three-legged German Shepherd, barking at the house. The dog possessed a remarkable sixth sense that transformed her into an outstanding police K9, able to sense danger before it even appeared.

Amidst the chaos of a frantic police chase, the unthinkable happened. Tiki was shot in the leg. The injury was severe, ultimately leading to her retirement from active duty. It took Elena months to navigate Mark's objections and finally adopt Tiki, but her determination paid off. This decision transformed both their lives for the better, forging a bond that would endure through the challenges they faced together.

No one thought a three-legged police dog would be

of much use. But for Hamilton Investigation and Security, Tiki was more than just a dog—she was a hero waiting for a second chance. They offered Elena an opportunity to reunite with Tiki in the field, as both prepared to fight for the greater good once more.

And they'd appointed her lead handler. Jesse Hamilton explained that each had a single handler to prevent overload. However, Jesse explained that there was an agent who had been acting as the lead handler and might need a gentle touch after the transition.

"Tiki, hier."

Tiki bounded over to Elena, her tail wagging with excitement. Together, they had practiced a series of commands in German, although Tiki was equally trained in English. They were ready for anything that might come their way.

As Elena left the driveway, she turned to Tiki, strapped into the passenger seat. "Tomorrow is a new day, girl. We'll unleash our potential and show the agents of HIS what we can accomplish together." She only hoped she would receive cooperation from the acting lead handler. Otherwise, her job would be difficult. Although she had been handling challenging situations with SWAT over the last few years, nothing could be worse than that.

As she sped away, she cast a final, intense glance at the tumultuous years behind her, her heart pounding. Suddenly, she slammed on the brakes, her eyes wide with shock. In the rear-view mirror, a blinding explosion erupted from Mark's home, sending a fiery plume into the sky.

Chapter Two

Kevin "Pup" Richards couldn't stand the nickname his teammates had slapped on him. Sure, he was the youngest in the pack, and yes, he was the one who took care of the dogs, but was there any reason to label him with such a childish moniker? Why not something cool and mysterious like "Bulldog?" Instead, he was stuck with "Pup," a name that felt more like a yelp than a title of respect. It was a constant reminder of his youth, and it just didn't sit right.

Every weekend, he and Casey—a spirited one-year-old Labrador—ventured to the dog park, determined to enhance the canine's social skills. Pup planned for her abilities to surpass those of the other team's canines and the two retiring HIS dogs. Bomber and Daisy were remarkable dogs, and Pup cherished every moment spent working alongside the two. However, as time passed, it became clear that these lovable companions were ready for a new chapter—a forever home where they could enjoy simply being.

Bomber. Now, that was a great nickname. Why

couldn't he have something more like that?

Once again, he mentally shrugged it off, balancing a large bag of dog food in one arm and Casey's leash along with grocery bags full of canned dog food in the other.

The early December air in Baltimore was a biting chill, a sharp reminder of winter's looming presence. He regretted the walk to the park and down the block to the pet store. He should've driven to avoid the brutal wind and forthcoming rain.

With his apartment building in sight, the two quickened their steps as raindrops pelted Pup's head. Unlike many of the men in HIS who had settled into cozy homes, he still clung to the independence of apartment life. A home, after all, felt more…permanent, a commitment he wasn't quite ready to embrace at twenty-five.

The word "permanent" sparked his thoughts about Doc's upcoming wedding. What on earth was he supposed to get them as a gift? She was a doctor, after all, and likely had everything one could imagine.

As Pup approached his building's front door, he felt relieved when someone opened it to exit. Raindrops fell more rapidly, each drop a harbinger of an impending downpour, and he braced himself for the inevitable deluge.

"Hold that, please." He couldn't dig into his pocket for his keys to unlock the door, so this was a godsend.

Instead, she closed the door and stood before the entry, under the awning, with her arms crossed.

"What the fuck?" He glared at her while shifting the bag of dog food in his arm so it wouldn't fall.

The woman he had seen at the dog park before stared back at him as if he had done something wrong. Didn't she have a three-legged dog? That wasn't a problem. He just liked to associate a human face with a dog.

"I'm sorry. I don't know you, and I won't allow someone who shouldn't be here inside." She knelt and reached for Casey. "Besides, for all I know, you could be a mass murderer."

Casey stepped up to the beauty and sniffed her outstretched hand.

"Casey," Pup warned, and the dog returned to her spot at his side. The rain poured down relentlessly, and he was fuming as the woman stayed dry under the overhang, leaving him drenched.

She stood, and he narrowed his eyes. "You don't pet working K9s when they're working." His anger rose as the weight in his arms seemed to double.

"I know that, but she's not working, right?"

How she knew that he didn't understand. For all she knew, Casey was his service dog, and she'd shut the door in his face.

She stepped away from him and opened an umbrella. "Besides, it says she's in training."

"Hey, wait." Pup's voice trailed to her retreating form as he stepped under the overhang, thankful for the relief of the waterdrops. "How do I know you aren't a mass murderer? I've never seen you before in this building." At the dog park, yes, but in this building, never.

She turned with a grin. "You don't." Then, she seemed to skip away.

Stunned by what had happened, Pup forgot about the weight in each arm, his wet clothing, and the dog. He would find out who she'd been visiting and speak with the tenant about her unwelcome behavior. This was beyond ridiculous.

He looked down at Casey, who watched the woman retreat, and wagged her tail. "Boy, oh boy. Whoever her man is will have his hands full."

Casey turned to him and let out an excited yip.

"Okay, let's get out of this rain."

He carefully set the heavy bag of expensive dog food on the stoop, taking care not to tear it and spill the contents.

Grumbling about having to go to such extremes, he realized his keys were in the other side of his jeans pocket. Now, cursing and directing his anger at the woman, he retrieved his keys, unlocked the door, and entered with Casey.

First, he set down the bags of canned food, then returned to the door to grab the rest before it closed and locked again. Thankfully, his apartment was the first one on the ground floor. It had once been the live-in landlord's place, so it was larger than the other apartments, and he loved it.

As he stepped into his apartment, he quickly set down Casey's food on the floor, then gently unbuckled her harness and slipped off her "K9 in Training" vest. With a swift motion, he grabbed a towel from behind the door, using it to dry himself off before giving Casey a refreshing wipe-down.

As the Lead Dog Handler for Hamilton Investigation

and Security, Pup knew he should enforce the rule about keeping the working K9s off the furniture, but how could he resist? Casey's infectious charm was irresistible. After all, the adorable troublemaker had unearthed her first real bomb at just six months old.

Even though he wasn't officially the "Lead" Dog Handler at HIS, everyone referred to him as such—after all, he was one of two dog handlers. He knew the Hamilton brothers were hunting for another handler, which would allow for one canine per team.

Before HIS, he was a Deputy U.S. Marshal who had only begun working with dogs a year after joining HIS. He felt capable of overseeing the program but knew others had more experience.

He shrugged mentally, adopting his carefree attitude. Whatever happens, happens. There was no use in stressing about it. He would still have Casey to work with.

His phone buzzed in his pocket. He hesitated, initially intent on ignoring it, but a second thought quickly crossed his mind—his team was on call. While he and Casey collaborated with all squads, even those in training, he was officially assigned to Bravo team and Grits.

Noticing the call was from Jesse Hamilton, the formidable leader at HIS, he quickly answered. "Hey there, Jesse."

"How's everything going, Pup?"

He shrugged with a wry smile, even though he was fully aware the man wouldn't catch it. "Just as good as ever." His boss wouldn't care about his run-in with a woman he'd never met.

"One thing I genuinely admire about you is your

unwavering positive attitude."

Uh-oh. He was directing that compliment at Pup. This could only mean one thing—Jesse was likely trying to let him down easy. He could sense it in the air. Nothing irked him more than this kind of soft approach. Just say it outright already. That was his mantra.

"I appreciate that."

"I wanted to let you know that we've found another handler, specifically for Alpha team. This handler and dog were part of Baltimore SWAT."

"That's great news." Someone from SWAT likely had more experience than he did. Shit. That was both a blessing and a curse.

"About the lead handler position—"

Pup's heart raced as he held the phone, hanging on every word. He tried to reassure himself that whether he secured the role or not, he'd be okay. But deep down, he knew the truth. He craved that position passionately. It wasn't just about a title. It was his chance to leave the shadows where the teams treated him like the kid on the block. After all, how could they take him seriously when he was the youngest among them?

"The other handler had far more experience."

"I understand." A heavy sigh escaped him at the thought of losing the role.

"I'm sorry, Pup. Learn from her, and we'll find a lead role for you somewhere in the organization. That, I promise."

"Really?" His voice broke with surprise, and he quickly cleared his throat. "Thank you."

"Just be ready. It's going to be quite the challenge.

She has a wealth of experience and a dog that's not just any dog—a certified hero."

Pup's heart raced. Sure, Alpha team would thrive under this addition. But what would she teach him?

"I strongly feel she'll put you through the wringer to assert herself as the superior candidate. So, keep your guard up."

"You don't trust her?" He wondered why anyone would hire someone they didn't fundamentally trust.

"Oh, I trust her wholeheartedly to get the job done. But I also trust that she's eager to prove herself."

"Do you think I'll like her?" Why did that matter? A boss was a boss.

Jesse laughed. "Oh, you won't just like her—you'll absolutely love her and her dog."

Pup scoffed. He wouldn't love any woman and her dog—well, maybe her dog. But women, they were—well, women. They were fun and sexually satisfying, but there were too many of them to "love" one.

"Thanks for letting me know personally, Jesse." Pup's voice was filled with genuine gratitude.

"Just remember, Pup, we're here whenever you need us."

Pup understood that "us" referred to the entire Hamilton family, but he instinctively knew he'd first reach out to his team leader before considering a jump to the big bosses. "Thanks again."

As they ended the call, Pup's gaze fell on Casey, who was eagerly staring at him.

Pup shook his head. "We didn't get it, girl." His heart felt heavy, and a strong emotion washed over him. It wasn't that he wanted to cry, but he was simply sad about losing the position.

Well, technically, he didn't lose the position. It was never his. He'd just stepped up and done what needed to be done.

Feeling let down, he retreated to his bedroom to shed his soggy clothes and take a shower. Just as he was perfecting his short-cropped hair, the door buzzer chimed, signaling the arrival of the group he anticipated.

His teammates had probably already heard the news and would be carrying cases of beer to commiserate with him.

He pressed the buzzer near his front door to unlock the building's entry door and allow the agents to enter.

Straightening his spine and reminding himself it was okay, he opened his apartment door for his guests.

During a lull in the storm, they each nodded to him as they strode past carrying boxes. Where were the men going, and whose boxes were they? He hadn't heard of someone moving in, but the apartment next to him had only become available yesterday.

Pup heard Casey whine beside him. "Go ahead."

With a joyful bark, she bounded over to Doc, the team's largest guy. The two had bonded about six months ago when Doc had been injured. The medic placed the box on the floor and petted Casey, whose tail wagged a mile a minute.

"We'll be right there." Doc hoisted the box and headed past Pup's apartment.

What the actual fuck was happening?

Curious, Pup followed the last of his teammates

down the hall and, sure enough, to the apartment next to his. He could only hope they weren't a loud family.

As he neared the door, he heard a woman's beautiful laughter and chuckles from the men. Making his way through the throng of men, now empty-handed but standing around, he thought to introduce himself to the new neighbors.

He froze when he finally moved to the front and into the living room of the apartment. He narrowed his eyes. "You."

Chapter Three

Elena stiffened at the voice before looking up from the vase in her hands. She knew he was a tenant, or else why would he have been so insistent about getting into the building with his dog and dog food? Burglars and mass murderers don't usually keep their arms full. They want to be able to escape at any cost.

She set the vase down, put her hands on her hips, and smiled. "So, you are a tenant." She didn't mean to sound snarky or bitchy, but something about this kid stirred her up.

Kid? What was he? Twenty-five or twenty-six. When did she start thinking of that age as a kid? She was only thirty-two. She inwardly groaned. God, she was getting old.

"Of course, I'm a tenant." After that snap at her, he looked around the room at the stunned faces of his colleagues. "What are you all doing?"

Cowboy looked down and scuffed his boot across the living room carpet. "We were just bringing boxes up for—"

"Good. Now that you're done, you can get your asses next door."

Elena raised her eyebrows at the boldness of this kid. The men were her new teammates, and Jesse had sent them to help her unload her boxes at her new apartment. He didn't say they were supposed to go next door afterward to visit.

"I think there might be some confusion. These men —"

"Whatever. They're my teammates and here to visit me, so they're done here. You can get whatever you have left on your own."

Elena heard a couple of the men inhale sharply. Wait, what? He was a teammate. Blood flooded her face. Was this the kid who had wanted the job she just took? He had a working K9 in training and had just identified her new teammates as his. And, she'd shut the door on him earlier…in the rain of all things. Oh, geez, this couldn't get any worse. She had to fix this.

Changing her tone and smiling, she stepped toward him and reached out her hand. Before she could introduce herself, he spun around and stormed out of the apartment. Okay, he wanted to act hostile. Unfortunately, she'd had plenty of practice at teammates doing that.

She turned to the man she thought was a team leader, though not her own. Her team leader, Boss, was on vacation with his wife and son. She'd already met him and liked him. This man—Grits, she thought—raised his eyebrows. "Um, what just happened?"

It took a moment, but Grits finally grinned, which totally confused her. "That was our very own Pup. He might be a little cranky right now because—"

He didn't have to finish that sentence. She knew it was because she got the job he coveted. Well, plus, she'd locked him out in the cold and rain.

Grits cleared his throat. "He received some bad news."

Elena closed her eyes. "This did not go well."

The man she easily recognized as Cowboy stepped toward her and removed his cowboy hat. "Not in the least."

Well, now wasn't the time to dwell on someone else's attitude. She had unpacking to do and a bare apartment to make homey because she refused to live as sterile as Mark had wanted their place to be. She wanted color, art, and throw pillows.

Cowboy returned his hat to his head. "We'd better get next door. I'd hate for him to think we didn't come for him in the first place."

Elena bit her lower lip. "Are you going to tell him the truth?"

Cowboy laughed. "Hell, no. I'd rather see his face tomorrow when Jesse introduces you and that K9 of yours." He looked around the apartment. "Speaking of which, when do we meet her?"

Jumping, Elena felt horrified. She'd left Tiki alone in one of the bedrooms so she wouldn't get in the way. "Hang on." Rushing to the room, she tried not to dwell on the men's plan to surprise the kid rather than prepare him. What kind of teammates were these?

Opening the door, Elena saw Tiki sprawled on the bed as if she owned it. "Tiki."

The dog jumped. It took only a moment for Tiki to bound to her, follow her into the living room, and go to each man for pets—greedy girl. "Guys, this is Tiki."

Elena watched the men love on her dog and laughed when Tiki dropped to the floor and gave Grits her belly to rub. "Sorry."

"What for?" Grits knelt and petted Tiki.

"She's a great working K9 and an attention hog."

The men laughed and looked at Cowboy.

Had she missed something? She had a lot to learn with this group, but the fact that they helped her move—even though Jesse had probably mandated it—warmed her heart. It was more than the SWAT men had done after she joined the team.

Cowboy put his hands up as if to ward off their glares. "Whoa, I ain't no such thing."

Grits stood. "Time to go, men." He turned to Elena. "I'd say let Pup know if you need anything since he's right here, but that won't work. At least, not yet."

Truer words hadn't been spoken to her today.

"In the meantime, call me while Boss is out of reach." He handed her a card that held only a phone number. "He should be back soon."

Tears threatened to well in her eyes. She would not cry. She would not cry. This was too much, though. It affected her emotionally and wasn't what she wanted the men to see on the first day—a blubbering mess.

"I wish he weren't cutting his vacation short just because of me." She had informed Jesse about the explosion, and he had promptly reached out to Boss, who was now rushing back from his getaway to assist her in

21

navigating the investigation with the Baltimore PD, despite her having more connections than he did. Yet, there was something undeniably heartwarming about it.

"We're not SWAT. We're a real team."

Nodding, she walked behind Bravo team leader as he left. Before she could close the door, she called Grits. "Do you think this situation is going to be a problem?"

She hadn't specified which situation, but she thought Grits understood her.

He shook his head. "The kid will get over not getting the job. Just give him a couple of days."

"Okay." She closed the door behind the Bravo team leader. I hope my team leader is as thoughtful. She'd yet to meet the Charlie team leader. Because the K9 program was under her direction, she would work directly with the three.

Even with the door closed, Elena could hear the men greet Pup next door. She bet he hated that nickname. She would. What would they begin to call her? Well, she couldn't worry about it now.

Moving to the living room, she dropped onto the couch and patted the seat beside her for the whining Tiki. "Yeah, I know." She petted the dog behind the ears. "They were nice." There had only been six of them, but that gave her an idea of the team camaraderie.

She nearly jumped off the couch, startling the dog. "The wedding, Tiki! I forgot to ask about it." Doc had invited her to his wedding, making it sound mandatory for the teams to attend. He'd given her the location and time, but was she just to arrive? Did she need an official invitation? What was the dress?

She had so many questions, but she'd be damned if she'd walk next door and interrupt the men with Pup. Especially since she found out he had been her competition.

Leaning back on the couch, she was lucky her friend Jennifer had found this place for her on a neighborhood site. She ran her fingers over the worn fabric and couldn't be prouder. It wasn't much, and she'd buy a new couch soon, but she had her life back—no more Mark.

The apartment had a lot of potential, and she loved that the owner allowed her to paint the walls. Of course, she had to repaint them before she left or forfeit her security deposit, but she could and would. Maybe the men would help her with that also?

Where were the female agents? She imagined they would have been there if they'd known about the move. It was last-minute, after all. She sighed. She'd meet them soon enough.

When it got louder next door, she guessed Pup was just trying to be an ass to pay her back. She hoped the other tenants weren't upset. Then again, maybe it was like this all the time. She hoped not.

Mindlessly rubbing Tiki's head, which now rested in Elena's lap, she wondered aloud. "I have no clue what to wear tomorrow. Oh, no. Do I have to get a present?"

As if in response to her wanderings, Tiki groaned.

"Hush, girl. It's an important thing to consider."

Believing they didn't expect her to have a gift since she'd only been invited one day prior didn't deter her. She always arrived with a gift in hand. "I've got to go, girl."

Elena ushered Tiki off the couch and grabbed her

purse and keys. She'd pick up something small so she wouldn't arrive empty-handed.

Walking past Pup's apartment, Elena stopped. Would they ever invite her to join them? Not Pup, per se, but the team?

She sighed and left the building. As she reached her assigned parking spot, her eyes widened. A truck was parked right behind her, blocking her in. Her frustration grew, but so did her curiosity. She approached the truck and looked inside, but the windows were dark—probably darker than the legal limit. Maybe it was one of the men who didn't have another place to park when they arrived.

Deciding it had to be done, she marched back into the building and knocked on 1A. The door whooshed open, and Pup stood there, glaring at her.

"Hi, again." Why was she nervous? He couldn't hurt her. But she had wanted to make a good impression on her subordinates when she began work. Well, that ship had sailed. "I think one of the guys—"

Before she could finish, Pup leaned against the doorjamb and crossed his arms. "I'm sorry, but were you attempting to go somewhere?"

Her mouth fell open. Son of a bitch. The little shit had parked behind her purposefully, probably to pay her back for not letting him into the building earlier.

Instead of engaging in what was sure to be an immature argument, she took a breath and grinned. Two could play at this game. She pulled her cell from her purse and clicked on a number.

"Hi, Sergeant Harper. This is Elena." She nodded at the inane chatter coming from the sergeant. "Yes, I'm doing fine. Listen, I need a tow truck at my new address. Someone abandoned a truck in the parking lot, blocking me in."

"You wouldn't."

Elena ended the call and dropped her phone back into her purse. She smiled broadly at one-upping him. "Oh, but I did."

Chapter Four

Pup had to talk quickly to prevent his truck from being towed to an impound lot. He couldn't believe his neighbor would go to such lengths. Then again, what he'd done was petty—very petty. It also revealed his immaturity. Yeah, he noticed she was older. Hot. And older.

He wondered about the crazy question from the cop. "Are you her stalker?"

How serious was this stalker? What kind of trouble was she in? Pup didn't go for that and figured he'd have to chat with her to ensure this stalker didn't broadside her. Sigh, he'd have to eat crow, he guessed.

As he lay in bed the next morning, he realized he hadn't gotten her name. He thought one of the agents said "Elena," but he couldn't be sure if it referred to her or someone else. He wanted to smack himself for not asking, but he'd been so enraged after discovering she was his neighbor—the same woman who refused to let him into the building.

He sighed and threw back the covers. Cold air struck his bare chest, raising goosebumps. He liked sleeping in a cool room, even in winter, but he reached for the thermostat and nudged it up to warm the apartment.

Heading to the kitchen, Pup thought more about the situation because it wouldn't leave his mind.

He figured she shouldn't let just anyone into their building, so he couldn't really blame her for that, especially someone with a stalker.

Did he just add "their" building? Well, he did. Unfortunately, he'd have to find a way to play nice with her. Who knew? Maybe she had younger, hotter friends he could meet.

That thought made him smile as he opened the refrigerator, grabbed a carton of orange juice, gulped several swallows, before putting it back in. He'd never developed a taste for coffee, so his usual morning drink was orange juice.

He scratched his bare chest and stretched. The room temperature began to creep up to a level that was satisfactory to him.

Sunday. What did he have today?

Pup snapped his fingers. "Doc's wedding." He decided there had to be a disease among some of the men. Since beginning at HIS, this was his fourth agent's wedding, and that was after the brothers' weddings. He shuddered at the possibility of catching the disease. That was something he needed to avoid.

He didn't oppose marriage, but he was only twenty-five. Wasn't he supposed to enjoy life before settling down in his thirties? That's what his father had ingrained in him from childhood. Of course, his mother and father had been high school sweethearts who'd had a baby nine months after senior prom.

Moving to the bathroom to shower and get ready for the day, Pup once again thought of the beauty next door —the pain in the ass beauty, but a beauty nonetheless.

In a moment of insanity, he considered inviting her to be his plus one for the wedding. Thank goodness the moment passed without incident.

While taking a long, hot shower, Pup's anger flared again as he thought about not being chosen as lead handler. He could brush it off, but the anger always returned.

Rubbing a towel over his wet skin, Pup looked in the mirror to see if he needed a haircut. He turned his head from side to side before wrapping the towel low around his waist. The sides were shaved close, and the top was just right to gel into place.

He whistled while rummaging through his clothes for the wedding. The ceremony was still hours away, but he might need to press something, so he didn't want to leave it to the last minute, as he often did.

Seeing an outfit ready to wear, he shoved his legs into jeans and zipped them up, but left the button undone. Who was he trying to impress? He lived alone. And, he liked it that way.

After a quick breakfast of cereal, an hour of scrolling through social media, and the rest watching sports highlights, Pup was ready to get dressed and leave. He'd see his colleagues there and could apologize for his rudeness and acting immature during their visit. So much for losing the nickname of "Pup."

He listened for any movement next door. So far,

she's been a quiet tenant, but it's only been one night. He would wait and see. Anything is better than the previous tenants and their loud children.

When his phone rang, he checked the screen and smiled. Accepting the call, he dropped onto the couch. "Hey, sweetheart. I was just thinking about you."

****

Elena yanked off the blue and white dotted pattern dress, feeling an instant sense of relief. She chose to slip into a pair of black slacks paired with a striking black and white blouse, opting for a look that felt more authentically her. She was all about comfort regularly—black cargo pants, casual T-shirts, and sturdy combat boots made up her daily ensemble. The frills and fluff of the dress just weren't her style.

She couldn't believe that her first time meeting the rest of the HIS teams would be at a wedding, but Doc suggested she attend and get to know the men and women "off the field." She knew it made sense, but her nerves….

As she stepped onto the scene, her eyes swept over the crowd, searching for Doc or Jesse. Weddings weren't her thing. Maybe it was the nagging reminder of her elusive search for "the one," the kind of connection that made her see stars when they kissed. And then there was the relentless ticking of her biological clock. At thirty-two, she realized she still had time to start a family, yet her heart seemed to race ahead, outpacing her thoughts, often leading her down paths of uncertainty.

To her relief, Jesse and his family approached her.

"Elena, it's my pleasure to introduce you to my wonderful wife, Kate, and our two amazing kids, Reagan and Jason." Jesse's proud smile lit up his face.

Elena managed a smile, hoping it didn't betray her unease. "It's a pleasure to meet all of you." She shook hands with each of them, feeling warmth from their welcomes.

Reagan stepped forward. "I get to stand in the reception line and introduce you to everyone." She infused her words with a dramatic flair that made Elena chuckle despite her nerves.

Then she caught what the preteen had said. Elena blinked, her heart racing. The reception line? "Wait. What? Sorry, what did you say?"

Jesse smiled and shrugged. "Yeah, we figured we'd kill two birds with one stone here. Doc and Julie thought it would be quicker for you to meet everyone if you were in the receiving line."

"Oh." A wave of surprise washed over Elena. She certainly hadn't anticipated anything quite like this. She had to decide how to get out of it. She wasn't opposed to meeting everyone, but in a receiving line? It put her on display, and she wasn't one for that attention. Hadn't she met enough of the team already?

"Really, it's okay. I don't want to take away from their day." Elena smiled genuinely, but it was tinged with uncertainty.

"Too late for that." AJ Hamilton strode over with a radiant woman at his side and two lively children in tow.

"Elena, meet my incredible wife, Megan, and our delightful duo—Ace and Pamela."

Elena felt a whirlwind of introductions as she eagerly shook hands and exchanged pleasantries with the remaining Hamilton families, mentally scrambling to remember the names. Typically, she prided herself on her memory, but the onslaught of new faces was a challenge she didn't anticipate.

Each introduction brought its smiles and chatter, but Elena secretly mused over how she would tell the twins apart. Brad and Matt were like mirror images, with similar features and styles, leaving her to ponder how she would navigate that little puzzle without getting tangled up in her confusion.

"It's such a pleasure to meet you all." She attempted to keep her energy high despite her internal chaos.

"You two." Megan laughed just as Pamela made a daring escape, her little legs propelling her toward the other children in a burst of giggles.

"Sorry about that." AJ chuckled, his eyes lighting up as he watched his wife sprint after their adventurous daughter. "My wife is faster than I am, so she's on chase duty today."

Elena couldn't help but burst into genuine laughter at the admission. She hadn't expected the "big, bad Hamilton brother" to show such vulnerability, which deepened her fondness for this lively family.

Reagan waved her hand. "All right, it's time to sit. I'm right here next to you." Her face was alight with excitement. "I've got all the inside scoop on the teams."

Kate put a hand on Reagan's shoulder. "Reagan, you know we don't gossip."

"Of course, Mom." Reagan raised her eyebrows at

Elena as if to say she had successfully placated her mother but was ready to spill the beans anyway. She gestured to Elena. "Come on."

Reagan guided her toward the back of the church, which Elena welcomed with relief. She didn't have to face the gazes of curious men and women, speculating about her presence. Instead, their eyes would meet hers individually in the receiving line—a more personal encounter that filled her with anticipation and dread.

As they settled into their seats, Reagan leaned in with a mischievous glint in her eye, her voice barely above a whisper, brimming with intrigue. "Dad said you met some of the team, but I'll just go through them all, just in case. That's Doc up front, and beside him is Grits. He leads Bravo team, though he's not the end-all leader. That title belongs to Boss, who's on vacation with Sugar and Cody. But, as you know, Boss also commands Alpha team."

Elena was drawn in by Reagan's whirlwind of words, hanging on every rapid-fire delivery. Was there even a pause for breath? No question was asked of her, so she merely nodded, feeling like she'd stepped into a whirlwind of names and titles that left her even more bewildered than before.

As the flower girls gracefully made their way up the aisle, a wave of anticipation rippled through the guests, their heads instinctively turning toward the back of the church. One sight captured Elena's attention among the unfamiliar faces—her new neighbor.

Learning he was with the team and one of her handlers, she expected to see him, but she was still nervous after their previous interactions.

Suddenly, their gazes locked, and he appeared taken

aback, his expression morphing into a mixture of surprise and irritation.

Leaning in toward Reagan, she lowered her voice to a whisper. "Reagan, do you see that man over there?" She nodded her head in her neighbor's direction.

Curiously, the preteen scanned the church pews, her eyes lighting up. "Oh, you mean Pup?"

She acted like she'd never seen him before and nodded. "I guess so. Is he a handler?"

Nodding, Reagan smiled. "Yeah, for Bravo team. Wait, you two haven't met? I'll introduce you first. He's a great guy."

Right. He's a great guy who blocked my car in a petty move.

Elena shrugged, as if not worried. "I'm sure I'll meet him later."

She sat on the edge of her pew, anticipation swirling in her stomach as the music continued. Instead of eyes fixated on the Maid of Honor gliding down the aisle, heads began to turn toward her, igniting dread within her. She fought the urge to hide, to cover her face and disappear into the fabric of her blouse. Yet amidst the chaos of attention, she felt a fierce determination bubbling up. She was stronger than the urge to shrink away, but the sensation of being on display was unsettling, almost... dirty.

Once her eyes focused on the bride and then the couple, Elena was immersed in the magic of the wedding. She jumped when someone leaned in and whispered in her ear.

"Why the fuck are you here?"

Chapter Five

Pup couldn't believe the audacity. His neighbor, having barely exchanged a few words with the men, dared to join the celebration. They'd only just moved a few boxes into her place, and yet there she was, acting as if she'd been part of the crew all along. What could possibly come next? No way she'd be crashing his get-togethers now.

When his whisper went unanswered, his eyes narrowed as he leaned in closer, drawn by an irresistible urge to inhale her captivating scent. Whether it was the lingering aroma of shampoo, the soft touch of lotion, or the allure of perfume, the woman's fragrance was intoxicating.

He attempted to be kinder this time. "Why are you here?"

Reagan leaned across his neighbor. "Shh, Pup. They're about to say the magic words."

He couldn't help but smile warmly at the girl. At eleven, she was still very much a kid, full of innocence and curiosity. He winked playfully and nodded gently, silently promising her that he was on her side and would do as she asked. Yet, he seethed at his neighbor.

Wait, did Reagan say "magic words?" The girl was quite the dreamer. That was obvious. Pup shivered when he heard Doc loudly proclaim, "I do!"

After the couple was pronounced man and wife, the room erupted in applause as everyone rose, with those nearby joining the celebration. He felt genuine joy for Doc, but a shadow of concern lingered. He couldn't shake the feeling that this unexpected guest might cast a pall over the special occasion. Was she just another wedding crasher, prone to overindulgence and embarrassing antics?

Pup pivoted to scrutinize her closely. He needed to be sure of her name. His gaze swept her from head to toe. No, she didn't fit the typical mold. Instead, she looked surprisingly tense in those close-fitting clothes that almost screamed FBI attire. Then, he wondered what she did for a living.

Why was his mind so consumed with her? It dominated his thoughts, relentless and unshakable. And yet, here she was—just beyond his reach, right in his backyard. A spark of defiance flickered within him. Maybe it was time to escalate their battle, to push her out of the event altogether.

The lively music floated through the air while men whistled playfully as Doc and Doc, quite proudly, strolled down the aisle, their smiles radiant and hands clasped tightly in a show of love.

When his neighbor tried to leave the aisle, he quickly grabbed her arm to stop her, feeling a sudden shock at her violent jump. His mind raced back to the comment about being stalked. Had she been hurt before? The tension in the air thickened as he wondered what secrets she might be hiding.

Reagan caught sight of him and huffed. "Pup, let her go. Elena's got people to meet."

He obeyed, yet a flicker of doubt gnawed at him. Why wasn't he one of those "people" his neighbor needed to meet? At least he had a confirmed name— Elena. He rolled it silently on his tongue, and a small, unexpected smile curved his lips. He liked it on her. But then, a jolt of confusion struck him. Why should it matter if it suited her? What was he even doing, caring about her name? Good grief, he was so furious with her that his thoughts tangled, making it hard to think straight.

Casper crept up silently behind him, catching Pup off guard as the agent's voice cut through the air. "What are you doing?"

Pup turned, blinking in surprise, and looked up at the towering figure of Casper. "What do you mean?"

Casper narrowed his eyes, a hint of suspicion evident. "You know what I mean. Why are you bugging Elena?"

Realization dawned on Pup—Elena had met Casper, too. He hadn't been around yesterday, so Pup wondered how they'd crossed paths. He shrugged cautiously. "I'm not bugging her. Just curious about why she's here."

When Casper's eyes suddenly widened, Pup's stomach tightened—something was definitely off. "What?" His heart pounded for no apparent reason, catching him off guard.

Casper hesitated for a moment. "You don't know, do you?" His voice was a mix of amusement and secrecy.

Pup sighed, frustration bubbling up. They always kept him in the dark, treating him like he couldn't handle the truth because he was so young. "Know what?"

Casper turned, a mysterious smile creeping onto his face, and his eyes flicked toward Nettie, Casper's wife, and Kayla, his surprise teenage daughter. He nodded subtly in their direction before facing Pup again. "You know what? I'll let you figure it out."

With that cryptic message lingering in the air, the agent spun sharply on his heels as he hurried toward his wife.

Pup's mind raced. What the hell was that supposed to mean?

"Hey, Pup!"

He shifted his gaze from Casper to a couple of teammates who had been at his place the day before. "Hey, guys."

A brief nodding acknowledgment swept through the group before Pup leaned in with a chuckle. "Can you believe my neighbor crashed the wedding? She just met you guys yesterday. I'm sure you didn't think she'd actually show up, yet here Reagan is, proudly introducing her around."

The men glanced away, fidgeting slightly, the awkwardness hanging in the air.

"What?"

"Nothing." Grits shook his head. "Just nothing."

Quickly shifting the subject, Romeo nodded toward the door. "What do ya think they've got for grub at this shindig?"

His mind was constantly buzzing with thoughts of

food, yet Pup was amazed he wasn't the size of a house. The secret lay in the agent's rigorous exercise regimen, like most on the team, including himself. Romeo, however, added a splash of adventure to his routine by surfing whenever the waves called.

"I hear there will be shrimp and crab, so I'm in." Grits slapped Pup on the shoulder. "Let's go see." He urged Pup forward into the aisle.

Guessing the men didn't want to broach the subject of Elena and how they'd fucked up in inviting her, he decided to let it go, for now.

"Grits, you'll eat anything seafood." Pup cast a quick glance at the other guests as they filed out of the small church. Doc's surgeon's wife had a circle of friends adorned in high-end clothing and glittering jewelry. Meanwhile, despite dressing well, Doc's guests would quickly ditch their ties when they stepped out of the church.

Thankfully, the reception was in a small building on church grounds. It also meant he couldn't ditch the party and cry "traffic or car trouble."

The men joined the long, bustling line of well-wishers stretching toward the reception. Having done this several times before, he knew the wait would be slow as each guest was eager to share heartfelt words with the bride and groom.

He could only say "congratulations," but even that didn't feel genuine. Why were the men rushing off to get hitched? Sure, he wasn't against marriage, but honestly, he was exhausted just thinking about buying more wedding presents. Next thing he knew, they'd be dragging him to coed baby showers filled with drooling toddlers—talk about an endless cycle.

Casper turned to the group. "I heard Boss is coming back early from vacation. I wonder if something's wrong with Alpha team."

Grits shrugged. "It's probably nothing to worry about."

But Pup wasn't convinced. He knew better than to jump to conclusions. Some things were just private, and the team leader wouldn't share unless he had to.

"Maybe he's coming back for the lead handler." Was it a flicker of hope—or was it curiosity—in his voice? He wondered if Jesse had said "her" or if he'd just imagined it. It didn't really matter. Pup had no problem working for a female lead. In the past, he'd done so without issue. After all, they put their pants on one leg at a time, just like him.

As usual, when he was nervous, he fell back on dog facts for others to learn. "Did you know some service dogs can open and close drawers? I want to teach Casey that trick."

The group groaned before the line moved forward, and they quickly followed behind.

Pup reached up and loosened his tie, a rebellious grin on his face.

"Stop." Cowboy strolled toward them with a calm but commanding presence. "Hold on until after you say congratulations to the bride."

Pup scoffed, crossing his arms. "Since when did you become the wedding expert?"

Cowboy adjusted his wide-brimmed hat, his eyes

twinkling with a hint of mischief. "When I got hitched, little buddy."

"Hey." Pup raised an eyebrow. "No need to be so mean about it." He hated it when Cowboy called him that. It always made him feel small, like he didn't matter. It reminded him how little they thought of him as an agent, young and green.

Cowboy chuckled, tossing his arm around Pup's shoulders with a grin. "Not mean at all. You know I've got a lot of love for you."

Pup rolled his eyes, stepping out of Cowboy's reach. "Gross."

The group burst into laughter, the kind that echoed around a room. They always laughed at him, and he wondered why he was the punchline this time. It wasn't like he'd told a joke or anything.

"Whatever." He put his back to them and turned toward the front of the line, then turned back. "Did you know that the police keep three-legged service dogs in service, even though they can't do everything?" He wasn't sure why he used the three-legged dog comment. Yes, he did. His neighbor was on his mind. When the men didn't groan as usual, he turned around toward the front, peering up at the line.

As they moved forward, the men eagerly swapped stories about their latest op—rescuing a kidnapped teenager. Pup hadn't been part of that operation, having been busy working alongside Alpha team as their handler during a high-stakes protection detail. He had used Bomber to sniff out the hotel room before the client arrived, but now, he's confident that Casey was ready to take on the task in the future.

The line hastened forward, urging them inward. As Pup's eyes gradually adjusted, he glimpsed the reception line stretching longer than he expected, though the thick darkness cloaked the figures beyond. It didn't matter— probably just Jesse and Kate waiting there.

Nearing the groom, he smiled. "Congrats, Doc. You did good."

Doc's face lit up with a bright smile as they clasped hands, sharing a quick, hearty man hug that spoke of camaraderie. "I did, didn't I?" The playful tone in his voice, full of pride and affection.

Pup shook his head and chucked. "Pity you had to get stabbed to meet her."

"Kid, you'd be surprised what you'll endure for the right woman."

There went the "kid" remark again. Maybe he'd never have their respect. Coming back to Doc's statement, he shook his head. "I'll have to trust you on that."

Doc laughed. "One day, Pup. One day."

Pup shook his head and moved to the bride. At least that "one day" wouldn't be anytime soon.

"Congratulations, Doc Julie." Pup hesitated, uncertain whether to stray from his usual gesture—an awkward handshake or a tentative hug. But Julie, with her warm smile, decided for him. She leaned in and pulled him into a reassuring embrace.

"Thanks for coming, Kevin."

Hearing his real name after so many calls of "Pup" felt surreal, and he often missed it. Still, he appreciated that she remembered. Smiling back, he managed a lighthearted reply. "Thanks for inviting me." What else was he supposed to say?

Turning to move into the reception, he noticed Reagan and Elena beside the bride. What the ever-loving hell?

Julie leaned in, a sly smile curling on her lips. "We thought it'd be easier—and faster—to introduce Elena this way."

Pup tilted his head, puzzled. Why go to such extremes for a stranger? Had one of the guys fallen for her yesterday?

Reagan beamed brightly. "There you are! I've been waiting all this time just to see you."

Pup nodded, though his eyes stayed fixed on Elena's rich, chocolate-brown gaze. They had just "seen" him in the church. What was different now? "Sorry to keep you waiting."

The preteen gestured warmly towards Elena. "Pup, this is Elena. She's the new lead handler at HIS."

And with those simple words, everything changed. His world suddenly collapsed around him.

Chapter Six

Elena couldn't believe the agents hadn't told Pup she was the new team member yesterday. She'd expected him to ask about her, yet he seemed oblivious. Did she think too much of herself?

Yet, he looked crushed and defeated. Was it because he lost the job to a woman? A Mexican woman? She quickly stopped herself—she didn't want to assume. Not everyone was like her bigoted SWAT teammates.

"Hi." She extended her hand, acting like they'd never had words. "It's great to finally put a face to the name."

Pup stood there, stunned, his gaze fixed on her.

She watched him carefully, a mixture of sympathy and frustration churning inside her. Despite his earlier behaviors, she couldn't help but feel a flicker of concern. She chalked it up to his age and apparent stubbornness— she'd long ago accepted that women tend to mature faster than men, and some men never quite catch up. She hoped he was the former, not the latter.

"Pup." Reagan's sharp whisper, edged with frustration, appeared to rouse him. "What's wrong with you? Shake Elena's hand. The line's backing up."

Elena broke eye contact with Pup and turned away. Sure enough, the queue had stalled, its attention fixed on them. As she began to retreat her hand, Pup moved faster, gripping hers with his big, warm hand and giving it a firm shake.

"I guess all's fair in love and war." A mysterious smile played on his lips before he dropped her hand and turned toward Reagan. He wrapped his arms around her in a comforting hug, whispering something in her ear that Elena couldn't hear.

What on earth was that about? Love and war? There was no love—attraction on her part, maybe. But love? Definitely not. Elena knew she had to smooth things over with Pup. She'd be one of his superiors, after all. She had to find a way to fix this before it spiraled out of control.

As the line moved forward, she warmly greeted each agent, and the introductions flowed much more smoothly than the awkward one with Pup. Finally, she met the two female agents, both proudly part of the new Charlie team. She was then informed that a new female helicopter pilot had been hired to join Bravo team. She appreciated the diversity and strength within her group.

As the line finally came to an end, she turned to thank Doc and Julie, her words bright with gratitude. Reagan gently guided her away before she could get too comfortable, reassuringly gripping her arm. She hadn't anticipated having an escort during the festivities, but deep down, she was thankful, especially since facing Pup alone again was the last thing she wanted right now.

Reagan called over her shoulder, her voice playful

yet persistent, nearly dragging Elena along. "Come sit with us."

Elena hesitated, unsure who "us" was, but decided to go with the flow. When they reached the kids' table, she paused, feeling a bit out of her element. Not that she disliked kids—she enjoyed their energy—it was just that she preferred adult company.

Suddenly, Jake Cavanaugh—the Hamilton foster brother—approached, eyebrows raised in concern. "Reagan, what are you doing?" He placed his hands firmly on his hips, as if ready to intervene.

Reagan turned confidently. "She's coming to sit with us."

Jake sighed heavily, shaking his head. "Oh, really?"

He eyed Elena, who shrugged helplessly. What was she supposed to do? She didn't want to hurt Reagan's feelings, but the eager eyes and curious ears at the kids' table made her feel torn.

Reagan looked at Elena, her expression hopeful. "See."

Jake shook his head. "But I need to talk to her, so she's sitting at our table."

Elena's smile was appreciative yet weary. She looked at Reagan with a mixture of amusement and resignation. "I'll come by later, and we can chat more." She couldn't hide her surprise at having said "chat" with a kid.

Still bubbling with energy, Reagan grinned and turned toward the table. "She'll be back." She flopped onto a chair, chattering excitedly with a younger girl Elena recognized as Amber, Jake and Emily's daughter.

As Elena drew closer to the large table, covered in a crisp white cloth, she slowed her steps. The wives were nowhere to be seen. For a moment, she hesitated to sit alone with all the Hamilton brothers—an uneasy prospect.

A flicker of worry crossed her mind—had they changed their minds because her dog only had three legs? But Tiki was capable, she was sure of it. She just needed to prove it.

Just then, AJ, the youngest Hamilton brother, glanced up from a chat with Jesse and smiled warmly. "Hey, Elena. Join us." His inviting tone made her feel suddenly welcomed.

Elena slid into a seat nestled between Jake and AJ, her eyes scanning the table where Jesse, Devon, Brad, and Matt were already seated, stoic yet smiling. Rumor had it there was another brother, but he was supposedly living out in Montana or somewhere far-flung like that. Elena couldn't wait to dive into the story behind it all.

Okay, so she did a bit of gossip here and there—nothing too scandalous, as long as it wasn't about her. Honestly, who didn't indulge in a little gossip now and then?

Brad's grin could melt hearts. "How was the meet and greet?"

She took a shaky breath, trying to steady her nerves. "It was fine." Her throat felt clogged and tight. Well, almost. Except for Pup, but she figured she didn't need to bring that up.

Emily, the ever-charming Hamilton sister, glided over to the table and effortlessly sank onto Jake's lap, her arm draped around his shoulders. She turned to Elena with a mischievous glint in her eye. "What's going on with Pup?"

Did they know about the petty squabbles at their apartment building? Probably not, but if Pup had shared everything with the other agents, it was possible. Emily decided to play it cool, acting as though everything was perfectly normal.

"I'm not sure what you mean." Elena shifted in her seat—a telltale sign she was hiding something. She couldn't help but wonder why it was so hard for her to lie convincingly. Most people seemed to master the art when it was in their best interest, but Elena's attempts felt painfully obvious.

Jesse shook his head, a hint of skepticism in his eyes. "That's not what we hear."

Elena internally groaned. So the male agents were a bunch of tattletales. She wondered which ones exactly, but quickly reminded herself they only had the team's best interest at heart. At least, that's what she kept telling herself to stay calm.

She shifted awkwardly. "We—" she glanced around the table "—haven't exactly started on the right foot." Her eyes darted nervously to the stern faces staring back. "But I truly believe we can work things out."

Devon drained his beer and leaned forward, his tone direct but not unkind. "Tell us what happened."

Well, there was no other choice. She had to reveal everything. She had to admit she'd been a bitch, and he'd been an immature brat. Would they understand? Honestly, she wasn't even sure she did.

"It all started the day I wouldn't let him into the building." She raised her hand to forestall any questions. "I'd just moved in and didn't realize he was a tenant. I wasn't about to let just anyone wander in."

The men nodded in understanding.

Emily smiled. "Of course not."

When she hesitated, AJ tilted his head, encouraging her gently. "What else?"

She took a deep breath, steadying herself before replying. "Did I mention it started raining?"

A collective groan rose from the table.

Elena didn't wait for a verbal response before beginning. "Then he found out I was his neighbor and that the agents were helping me move. I'm not sure if he realized that exactly, because he seemed to think they were there to visit him, but he definitely wasn't pleased."

Jesse nodded thoughtfully, a hint of exhaustion shadowing his face. "That must have been after I talked to him about the position." He wiped his face with his hand. "Sorry to put you in that tough spot."

Elena shook her head with a soft chuckle. "Oh, it gets worse." She quickly stilled, questioning why she'd shared so much. They didn't need to know the full story.

Devon raised an eyebrow, intrigued. "Oh?"

"Well, it was just petty stuff, but we're good now. The real issue was that he didn't know I was the new lead handler until the reception line. Let's just say it didn't go over well."

She scanned the room. Her gaze settled on Pup leaning against the wall, a beer bottle in hand, glaring at her while chatting with a few agents. Who were the extra women hanging around? Where had they come from? They didn't seem to be agents, and they looked young, just like Pup.

Internally sighing, Elena wondered why she even cared.

Women always seemed to surround mysterious men, and the agents had that allure in spades.

Jake leaned in to kiss his wife on the temple. "Do you think this will be a problem?"

Before she could respond, Matt spoke up, his voice steady. "We like Pup. We'd hate to see him uncomfortable, and we worried that not giving him the lead handler position might do that. But now, with all this…."

Were they second-guessing their decision to hire and promote her? She'd fight tooth and nail to keep this position, especially after already leaving the force. She and Tiki could handle this.

"I promise it won't be a problem." She smiled confidently at the family. "It's just a bump in the road. We'll be fine." Her words sounded reassuring, but inside, she harbored doubts. After Pup's reckless truck stunt, Elena wasn't sure about his maturity level, but she desperately hoped his professionalism would shine through for the job ahead.

"All right." Jesse nodded. "What do you need from us that we haven't already discussed?"

They had covered a lot, including the training field upgrade that the brothers promised her. She shook her head, a trace of unease in her system. "I can't think of anything else." Then she considered one thing. "Except to ask—please let me build that relationship with Pup. Don't interfere." She knew that if she didn't have that space, it would sound like she was tattling, which was the last thing she wanted.

The men and Emily exchanged glances around the table before Jesse nodded decisively. "Okay, but if any issues crop up, we're stepping in. We like you, Elena, and we're genuinely excited about what you can bring. But let's be clear—Pup stays in the picture. No exceptions."

A flicker of doubt crossed her mind. Did that mean she'd lose her job if Pup wasn't happy? The thought stung. As much as she tried to brush it off, unease bubbled inside her.

"I understand." Her skin prickled with anticipation, itching to leave the room. After the explosion, an unsettling feeling lingered in her mind—had the police discovered her stalker, too? As the prime suspect, it seemed inevitable they would. He wasn't a relentless pursuer, just a creepy figure who occasionally sent shivers down her spine. Each time she got close to unmasking him, he vanished, leaving her to chase elusive shadows. Determined, she vowed to solve this mystery herself— unless the police beat her to it.

Now wasn't the time to dwell on it. She had a job to salvage. She pushed herself to stand, hoping the conversation was finally over, and nodded politely around the table. "Thanks again for the opportunity."

AJ waved her off with a grin. "Say nothing about it. Now, go enjoy the party. The other agents are eager to get to know you better."

As she turned to walk away, she pushed aside her

doubts and left the group, noticing Reagan and Amber calling her over with cheerful waves. She sighed, wondering if sitting with the kids might help. It might be her chance to avoid Pup a little longer until she figured out what to say to smooth things over.

She shot another glance his way, but he wasn't looking at her this time. Instead, he was laughing at something a stunning woman said before whispering into her ear, her delicate hand resting lightly on his chest. His tie was loosened, a few buttons on his shirt undone, and each shift of light skimmed across the hard planes of his chest.

Her heart pounded fiercely as a swirl of confusion and curiosity took hold. He'd finally shed the hostility, laughing and enjoying himself. Wasn't that what she'd wanted for any subordinate? So why did a strange pang of unease ripple through her at the sight of his unrestrained joy?

Chapter Seven

Pup groaned and pressed his aching head. Why did he let himself get so wasted at the wedding? It had been ages since his last bender, and that was definitely the worst place to indulge. Honestly, he barely remembered the evening at all.

He rolled over in bed, anxiety creeping in. What if he did something stupid last night? As he tossed his arm across the mattress, it landed on something soft. Uh-oh. His heart skipped a beat. Please be someone he knew. He didn't recall bringing anyone home, and he hated that fuzzy, frustrating feeling of forgetfulness—especially when it came to names.

So, he'd been the reckless type last night. Who wouldn't be at his age? But lately, even that reckless streak was wearing thin. Maybe it was time for a change.

"Mmm." The soft purring voice caused him to gradually withdraw his arm, trembling slightly.

Pup edged silently off the bed, his heart pounding with a mix of relief and curiosity as he scanned the bed. There she was—Mona, his go-to gal. No strings, just their unspoken understanding, and both valued it that way. But a nagging question lingered. How had he ended up with her? She hadn't been at the wedding. Had she?

He couldn't quite remember. He slipped into the bathroom and looked in the mirror, grimacing at his reflection, which appeared haggard and worn out. Today was a busy day. Casey's training session was this morning.

His stomach sank as he thought of Elena. Had he said or done anything the night before that might have damaged their relationship further? A wave of unease washed over him, making the morning feel even heavier.

Well, he guessed he'd find out soon enough. After using the facility, he washed his hands, splashed cold water on his face to wake himself up, and quickly wrapped a towel around his waist before stepping into the bedroom.

Mona was there, dressing with a playful smile. "Why are you covering up now? I've already seen it all."

Pup scratched his bare chest and winced, feeling a strange heaviness today. Why did their faux afterplay seem so dirty today?

When Pup hesitated to join in the lively banter, Mona, now fully dressed and sitting on the edge of the bed as she slipped into her heels, turned to him with a curious smile. "What's wrong, Kevin?"

There it was—his name again. Mona had never liked the nickname "Pup" and had stubbornly pressed him until she finally revealed his real name. Sometimes, he wished he could go back to hiding behind that playful alias.

He shrugged, trying to hide his vulnerability. "Nothing. Just hungover."

Mona chuckled, teasing. "I bet. You were three sheets to the wind when you called me."

He glanced away, a faint smile creeping onto his face. So, he had called her. Probably because he was desperate for someone to talk to and break his unhappiness.

Only, it hadn't worked. Whatever secrets they'd exchanged the night before faded from his mind as if erased by an unseen hand.

Standing abruptly, Mona ran her fingers through her wavy, golden hair, a hint of curiosity in her eyes. "By the way, who is this Elena you kept prattling on about?"

Pup froze, tension tightening his muscles. He'd spoken of Elena. What had he revealed? Trying to mask his unease, he shrugged casually. "She's a new teammate and the lead handler."

Mona chuckled softly, a teasing smile playing on her lips. "I got that last night. And I'm sorry you didn't get the position."

He shrugged once more, feeling the throbbing headache cloud his thoughts. Could he do anything but appear nonchalant? "Thanks." Inside, he felt a swirl of conflicting emotions.

"Don't worry. Nothing happened last night."

Thank the fuck for that. He didn't know why, but he knew it was time to let this relationship go.

Walking Mona to the front door, Pup paused, a strange heaviness settling in his chest. He felt like he owed her more—perhaps an apology. In the living room, he came to a sudden stop, halting her steps. Turning slightly away, he hesitated. "Look." He swallowed the lump in his throat. "I'm sorry."

Mona raised an eyebrow, studying him. "For what? You did nothing wrong last night."

Relief flickered through him, but was gone in a heartbeat. He'd let his words slip about Elena, and now he felt exposed. He shrugged, trying to dismiss the tension. "I'm just—I'm sorry." A mix of regret and uncertainty lingered in his tone.

Her eyes widened. "Is this really goodbye to what we've shared?" Her voice broke on the last word.

Had it been? Maybe it was finally time to let go and seek a relationship that offered stability. He swallowed hard at the thought. Last night, he'd felt the love with the men and their partners—each of them seemed so at peace, so content.

Pup ran a hand through his hair, eyes clouded with uncertainty. "I don't know."

Mona stepped closer, her hand resting gently on his chest. She leaned in and kissed his cheek. "Figure out what it is about Elena that drives you crazy, then call me."

After Mona left, Pup walked back to the living room where Casey waited. He silently hoped that in his drunken haste, he'd remembered to walk her last night.

Suddenly, Casey leapt off the couch, barking joyfully and wagging her tail with uncontainable excitement. But before he could breathe a sigh of relief, a loud, thunderous bark echoed from next door.

Oh boy. He knew all too well—if those hounds kept barking back and forth, the neighbors would be none too happy.

"Shh, girl. Let's get you some fresh air." He hoped it

would clear his restless mind.

As Elena sometimes used the same dog park he frequented, he decided on a casual stroll instead, letting Casey explore and sniff her way around the block.

"Sorry about the park, girl. I'm just not ready to face her."

After the crisp morning air, a quick, refreshing shower cleared his mind and stoked his determination to start the day anew. He slipped into his black cargo pants and T-shirt, took a few moments to feed Casey, brushed off the brief conversation with Mona, sipped his invigorating orange juice, and nibbled on a protein-packed breakfast bar. Now, he felt ready to face whatever lay ahead.

"Are you ready, girl?"

Casey seemed to stand taller as he clipped the K9-in-training harness and leash onto her. With her tail wagging eagerly, threatening to knock over everything on the living room tables, he led her toward the door, every step filled with anticipation.

He was irritated by his petty comeback, which involved blocking her SUV, but he knew he should be the bigger person, let it go, and start fresh.

As they stepped out of the building, a sudden flurry of movement caught his eye. Elena was frantically tearing apart her car, tossing belongings onto the grassy edge of the parking lot. Meanwhile, her three-legged dog whined softly, restless on the grass.

Intrigued, Pup and Casey cautiously approached, keeping the dogs apart since the other handler was momentarily distracted. But then Casey halted abruptly and plopped down near the SUV, instincts kicking in. The whine in her voice told him she'd caught the scent of—drugs.

At that moment, Elena looked up from the back seat, seeing him and Casey in the act. "Yep, Tiki scented it too." Her eyes scanned him and Casey critically.

She stepped closer, her gaze equal parts curiosity and challenge. They were dressed similarly—black tactical gear—though her sleek, form-fitting clothes suited her better than his.

His nerves tightened. "What's happening?" He struggled to keep his tone steady. Was she testing his dog right away? Still, he knew Casey was quick to learn, capable of picking up on things faster than most. The tension in the air was thick, and he couldn't shake the feeling that something big was about to unfold.

Elena threw her hands on her hips, her voice slipping into Spanish—a language he didn't quite catch. Damn, she looked so damn sexy when she did that. Wait, what was he just thinking? Nope, not going there. "What?" He tried to shake off the distraction.

She waved a dismissive hand. "Never mind. Someone must've slipped drugs into my car. I guess the police are probably on their way right now."

He furrowed his brow. "Why would someone do that?"

She shot him a sharp look. "Why indeed? Now, be a hero and check the trunk. Rip everything apart."

Pup settled Casey on the grass away from the other dog before reaching into the open hatch. Elena and Pup continued their work silently, as if no tension or past incident had ever clouded their interaction. Suddenly, Pup paused, eyeing a small stash of drugs hidden in the lining between the rear of the vehicle and the back seat. His brow furrowed, and he hesitated before asking, "Why—" but his words were swallowed by a blaring police siren.

Two cruisers flashed their lights, approaching rapidly.

Elena's eyes widened in alarm. "Shit. Get rid of those before they arrive. I'll distract them."

He didn't question her reasoning. Instead, he retrieved Casey and returned to his apartment, and flushed the drugs down the toilet.

It was day one with his new supervisor, and he was already committing a crime. In his living room, he gave Casey free rein inside the apartment before stepping outside.

Three police cruisers and one K9 unit circled Elena's car, a dog sniffing eagerly at the trunk. Just as she'd suspected, trouble was brewing. But what the actual fuck was going on?

He tried to move closer to Elena, but a police officer stepped in, blocking his path. "She's my neighbor." As if that alone justified his approach.

"Stay back, sir. We're busy right now."

Peering around the officer, he smirked. "I see that. You know—" he glanced back at the tall man "—my dog could do that."

The officer rolled his eyes, exasperated. "Sure thing, buddy. Now, either head back to your apartment or take a hike. Just stay away from this area."

Pup hesitated, then flashed a fake smile. "But...that's

my ride to work." He lied through his teeth, attempting to sound innocent.

Catching his words and glancing again at his attire, the officer's voice sliced through the tension. "So, you work with Elena?"

Pup nodded, a flicker of defiance sparking inside him. He didn't fully understand why, but he wanted to ruffle the feathers of these people who mocked Elena. "Yeah, she's my boss."

The officer's eyebrows shot up beneath his patrol cap in disbelief. "Boss? Elena?" He chuckled mockingly. "No way."

That comment ignited Pup's temper. His relationship with Elena was complicated, but no one mocked another of HIS agents. Narrowing his eyes, he leaned slightly forward, warning the officer with a steely glare. "She's the lead dog handler for Hamilton Investigation and Security."

The officer froze. "Say what?"

It was obvious these men hadn't kept up with her latest role. Well, he'd make sure they knew she was more than just a part of the K9 units—she was a force to be reckoned with.

"Yeah." He gave the officer a confident smirk. "She's over the K9 units for the entire company." Pup hesitated for a moment, uncertain if the officer truly knew the scope of HIS or its size, but he made sure to emphasize her position as something big—bigger than they'd expect, bigger than it probably really was.

"HIS, you said?" His voice was tinged with disbelief as he shifted restlessly from foot to foot. The tension in the air crackled like static.

So, HIS truly did strike fear into crooked law enforcement officials. Good. Pup decided to play it up to the fullest. "Yeah, she's supposed to meet with the company president in"—he glanced at his watch—"about fifteen minutes." He fixed the officer with a mischievous grin. "Looks like you've made her late. That's gotta suck for you."

The officer spun around, eyes fixed on her SUV, where chaos was rapidly unfolding. "Stay here."

Pup almost chuckled as the officer hurried over to the K9 officer, exchanging hushed, urgent whispers. The officers exchanged glances—some uncertainty flickered across the K9 officer's eyes—and he shrugged.

Within moments, Elena and her dog were completely alone. The police convoy vanished as if by magic.

Pup stepped forward, his gaze steady. "Friends of yours?"

"You could say that. What did you tell them to get them to leave? I saw you talking to the officer."

Pup shrugged casually, a sly grin spreading across his face. "Oh, I just told them who you work for." He winked.

She laughed softly. "I didn't realize it was that easy."

Smiling mischievously, Pup leaned in slightly. "You'd be surprised at the clout HIS has here."

Elena reached down, gently petting her dog. "This is Tiki."

Pup crouched down to greet her. The dog sniffed his hand, then wagged her tail as he gave her a gentle pet.

"Now." Elena had a spark in her eye. "Go get your K9 and let's get to work."

Pup bristled at the command. She had seemingly forgotten she'd asked him to commit a crime a few moments ago. What the hell was he to do with this woman?

Chapter Eight

On the drive to the compound, Pup was at a crossroads, uncertainty clouding his mind. Should he confide in HIS about Elena and the drugs, risking her position? For all he knew, those drugs belonged to her, and she might have had a heads-up of the search. It wasn't far-fetched—she still had police connections, like the officer who threatened to tow his truck.

The stakes were higher than ever, and Pup felt the weight of the decision pressing down on him.

If HIS fired Elena, Pup's chance of becoming Lead Handler would finally be within reach. It was everything he had dreamed of—yet, he hesitated. Could he really climb to the top by sacrificing his integrity? The tension between ambition and morality pulsed in his mind, making the path forward anything but clear.

Then, a nagging doubt crept into his mind. Were the drugs truly planted? Regardless, she had received that critical warning of the search.

Pup's mind flashed back to the suspicion and hatred in the officer's eyes when he'd mentioned Elena's name, like she had been a target. Who had she crossed to provoke such animosity?

He shook his head, realizing she might not be the innocent victim he'd initially thought. A heavy sigh escaped him as he grappled with the truth. Trust was fragile, and right now, he wasn't sure he could count on Elena.

Turning into the HIS compound, Pup's eyes caught sight of another man walking a German Shepherd— maybe Charlie team's handler. If it were, he wouldn't be alone with Elena, and right now, he needed that. Despite their lingering angst, they had to talk about what happened. She couldn't dodge the subject forever.

After parking and releasing Casey from the truck, he surveyed the area. Where was she? More importantly, where did she want him and Casey to go?

Jesse stepped out of headquarters and hurried straight toward him. Uh-oh. What trouble had he stirred up now?

The two exchanged firm handshakes.

Jesse broke the silence. "Elena shared what happened."

Pup's eyes widened in surprise at the bravery he hadn't expected from her.

"Thanks for helping her." Jesse nodded. "It goes against everything we believe in terms of the law by discarding evidence, but it was the right call at the time."

Pup hesitated, glancing at the ground, then back at Jesse, his brow furrowing.

"Go ahead, say it."

Pup hesitated. "What if they were really hers?"

Jesse tilted his head, curiosity in his stare. "Do you

believe that?"

Pup stammered, unable to find the words, feeling the weight of his conflicting thoughts—something new even around Jesse. Elena, the woman who had haunted his life from the first moment, now seemed shrouded in mystery.

"I honestly don't know what to think."

"Pup—" Jesse started, then paused, his eyes locked onto the man Pup had spotted upon arrival. Pup followed Jesse's gaze.

As the man approached, Jesse extended his hand, greeting the stranger with a firm handshake.

Pup's interest piqued, and he stepped closer.

"Pup, this is Daylan. He's not been given a nickname yet, but I expect Charlie's team to catch up soon."

The mention of Charlie's team made Pup's ears perk up. They were an enigma, cloaked in secrecy, their training a puzzle everyone wondered about. Why the concealment? Why meet the handler face-to-face now?

Pup reached out first. "Nice to meet you." He gave a friendly shake. Then he glanced at Daylan's dog. "And what's your K9's name?"

Daylan looked down at the K9, then back at Pup with a warm smile. "This is Buddy."

"Long-time partners?"

Daylan grinned. "Since he was a pup." Daylan looked at Pup with wide eyes. "Sorry, man."

Pup waved him off. Calling a K9 a pup was utterly different than calling a human one. He could take it. At least that's what he wanted this stranger to believe.

"He's mine—completely."

A sting hit Pup's chest. Casey was a HIS dog, and although Pup was allowed to take her for training, deep down, the ownership still stung.

"Daylan, you'll soon meet the new Lead Handler. Elena comes with a formidable background working with K9—"

As he spoke, Pup's mind drifted to Casey. He'd have to find a way to adopt her—or get himself a puppy to train. One that was truly his, a partner he could call his own.

"—and her dog—"

"Tiki."

Jesse nodded at Pup, a glimmer of approval in his eyes. "Yes, Tiki will be perfect for today's training. I think you're going to like Elena and her training plan. You're in good hands."

He turned to leave, then paused, spinning back around. "Pup, we'll finish that conversation later today."

Pup simply nodded. What choice did he have? Saying "no" wasn't an option.

Suddenly, Daylan turned, curiosity etched on his face. "Did I interrupt something?"

Pup looked him in the eye and shook his head. "No." Although this was another HIS handler, he was essentially a stranger. Plus, it wasn't his place to disclose Elena's run-in with the law.

They allowed the dogs to greet and sniff each other, which helped them become comfortable with each other in case they were called to work together. When the release and play commands were given, the two dogs erupted into playful circles, chasing each other joyfully. It was heartwarming to see Casey genuinely play.

Daylan scanned the area. "So, where's our boss?"

Pup shrugged and then spotted her and Tiki walking toward them from the kennels. She must've just visited Bomber and Daisy—although, wait. Those two were now house dogs living with Jesse's family, no longer in the kennels.

Curiosity piqued. Maybe she was just checking out the facilities. But wouldn't the kennels have been one of her stops during the interview tour?

Or, a mischievous thought flickered. Was she hiding a stash of drugs there since they were now empty?

He chastised himself for the crazy idea. Besides, he'd flushed the drugs. His stomach clenched at how much trouble he could have been in if one of the officers had caught him in the act.

Attempting to brush it off, he nodded toward Elena. "There she is."

Daylan furrowed his brow. "Her dog is missing a leg."

"Yep."

Daylan turned back to Pup, a hint of concern in his voice. "How will she attack?"

Pup shrugged, just as puzzled. "Guess we're about to find out."

"Casey, heel." Pup's voice was sharp with authority.

When Daylan repeated the command for Buddy, the two dogs immediately ceased their activities and sprinted toward their respective owners. Well, handlers, since Pup wasn't truly an owner.

"Hi." Elena approached and offered a friendly smile.

"You must be Daylan." She extended her hand, her eyes hopeful. "It's nice to meet you."

Daylan nodded, shaking Elena's hand. "Yeah. You, too."

"This is Tiki." A sparkle of admiration rose in her voice. "She's an actual hero with an award and everything."

Pup swallowed the whoop-de-doo and kept his mouth shut. A twinge of jealousy pricked him anyway. Casey still hadn't been given a shining moment.

"This is Buddy." Daylan gestured to the eager dog.

Elena nodded at Buddy, then turned her gaze to Pup. "You made it." The surprise in her voice caught Pup off guard. Why wouldn't he have made it?

He simply nodded in return. "Yeah. We did."

"Let's head over to the K9 training field." Elena turned toward the sprawling area.

Pup and Daylan followed closely, their dogs trotting effortlessly beside them. When they reached the impressive K9 training zone—carefully crafted with a small fortune—their dogs' tails wagged in excitement.

Pup couldn't help but smile. Casey had already set a blazing record on the obstacle course, and he was confident she'd outshine Buddy and Tiki. Or at least, he hoped.

Elena faced the men with a grin. "Now, let's see what your K9s can do. Daylan, you're up first. I want to watch Buddy conquer that course."

Daylan nodded eagerly and stepped forward, Buddy trailing happily at his side.

Although everyone carried leashes, they usually let

the dogs run free here, and Pup loved those moments of unleashed joy for all of them.

Pup wanted to confront Elena about the morning's events, but she was entirely consumed with Daylan and Buddy.

Frustration simmered inside him. He had to set things straight.

As a Deputy U.S. Marshal, Pup had faced danger with fearless resolve. But lately, everything felt off. The bright start at HIS had given way to this tension. Suddenly, Elena Raymundo appeared on his doorstep—literally. Enough was enough.

He took a deep breath. "About this morning—" He hesitated to find the right words.

Elena glanced at him briefly before returning her focus to the course. "What about it?"

Pup's stomach clenched. "What about it? You had me flushing drugs down the toilet to hide them from the cops." His voice rose at the end words.

Elena's eyes snapped wide in surprise, but she didn't meet his gaze. "Keep your voice down. Thank you again, by the way."

It wasn't what he wanted to hear. Frustration boiled over. "Were those your drugs?"

Elena turned to him, her gaze cool and composed, causing his muscles to tense involuntarily. He wasn't bracing for a blow, but sensed she might give him answers he didn't want to hear.

"Does it matter?" Her voice was calm but piercing.

"Does it matter? Does it matter? Hell, yeah, it matters." He nearly shouted, frustration bubbling over.

How could she be so nonchalant about everything? If she hadn't been warned about the search, she'd already be in jail, fighting to get out with the Hamilton family's help—because, no matter what, HIS is HIS. Their motto, "We've got your six," wasn't just for the team. It seeped into every part of life.

She studied him for a moment, her eyes glinting with something indefinable. He was caught in the depths of her dark eyes, and suddenly realized just how much he desired her. But trust? That was another story. She was older than him and his boss, yet he couldn't shake his feelings.

Then he reminded himself—intimacy and relationships weren't the same.

"Just leave it." She returned her gaze to the course.

Pup shook his head, voice heavy with unresolved conflict. "I don't think I can."

Chapter Nine

Elena couldn't believe her ears. This kid was daring to question her integrity. Did Pup really think the drugs had been hers? She knew their start hadn't been smooth, and honestly, she almost snorted aloud at how mild that sounded. Still, she was determined to fix things so they could work together without more of these awkward confrontations.

"We'll discuss this later." Relying on her sense of authority, not her official position, but her word and presence, she kept her voice calm.

Pup took a visible deep breath, and she wondered if he'd hold it and then throw a tantrum. She mentally shook her head. He didn't deserve that low blow.

"Okay." He nodded slowly. "Okay."

Thank God. She really didn't want this conversation, but sometimes, you had to face the storm. And right now, she needed to focus. She was supposed to evaluate these two men and their K9 partners, after all.

Turning back to the course, Elena softly touched the whining Tiki. She always seemed to notice even the slightest shifts in Elena's emotions, and her dog's worried whimper warmed her heart. Elena's sharp gaze caught Buddy's hesitant pause before entering the tunnel. It was a subtle hesitation, but she had seen it. That small doubt could spell trouble in the field. She mentally noted it, adding it to her mental checklist of his training cues.

Daylan expertly commanded his K9, his tone firm yet confident, and the dog responded instantly—proof that he was a natural in the field. Jesse had promised he'd be an asset, and he certainly was. Yet, from what she gathered, she wouldn't get to work closely with him. His team was reserved for the high-stakes, covert missions—missions she craved. It was frustrating, but she understood. The organization prioritized what worked, not just the desires of one eager female.

When Daylan and Buddy finished the course, Daylan gracefully knelt, praising his eager dog with a warm smile and offering him a sturdy rope toy. Buddy barked joyfully, shaking the toy with excitement before settling into a comfortable chew. Daylan stood confidently and composed, yet uncomfortable.

Did he expect her to criticize him? If he disliked being evaluated, this wasn't the right field, because evaluations are simply part of ensuring the team's top performance.

"Good job." She nodded and smiled, though she secretly wished she'd timed them—maybe another day. Her nerves about being alone with Pup had distracted her, and it had slipped her mind.

"Thanks." Daylan's voice was steady and calm, despite just running the course with his K9 partner.

Impressive. She tilted her head curiously. "How

many times have you run the course?"

A bright, proud smile lit up Daylan's youthful face —what is it with these young handlers? "First time."

At that moment, she was genuinely impressed with Daylan and Buddy's teamwork, realizing they had potential that could shine even brighter in this challenging environment.

Elena turned to Pup, who watched them with bright curiosity, his eyes shimmering with anticipation. She couldn't quite grasp why, but Pup's gaze held a strange familiarity she couldn't put into words. "You and Casey are up."

Pup nodded confidently and squared his shoulders. "Casey, heel." He had allowed her some relaxation during Buddy's run. The moment he spoke, the loyal dog leapt to his side, eyes shining as she looked up eagerly. "Are you ready, girl?"

The K9 barked happily and wagged her tail furiously, ready for action.

It was clear they'd tackled this course many times before—enough for Casey to be familiar with it. Elena wished she'd timed Buddy, thinking it might help her gauge Casey's progress better. But since she hadn't, she'd need to pay close attention to how well Casey remembered the route. If she relied on memory rather than treating this as a challenge, Elena would have to get more creative with her training approach.

Pup turned to Daylan. "Let us show you how it's done."

Elena didn't find boasting appealing, yet she realized many men did it constantly. She silently hoped this wasn't just his normal behavior because it was a turn-off.

She stiffened slightly, a flicker of attraction crossing her mind. He was undeniably cute, but so was Daylan. Still, they were young men—probably not quite ready for a mature woman. She shrugged mentally, a little amused. Maybe they'd prove themselves mature someday, but that wasn't her concern. Her focus was clear. She was here to train their K9s, nothing more.

Daylan chuckled at Pup's boast and swung his arm, giving Pup free rein of the course. With that, the K9 and handler strode away, and Elena watched eagerly as they headed straight into their next adventure. That's how she liked to see them.

"Did you time us?"

Her eyes stayed fixed on the duo, and she shook her head with a tight-lipped smile. "Not this time. We'll do that on the next run."

Daylan huffed, and Elena nearly rolled her eyes. She didn't want to feel competition between these two men, but a flicker of worry sneaked in. Her goal was clear. She was to build a team that outshone any other agency's K9 unit. These dogs weren't just for show. They searched for drugs, bombs, people, anything that could serve the organization's mission.

"Are you ready?" Pup's voice was clear and commanding as he took his position alongside Casey.

Elena nodded, grateful that the sun was behind her, casting a protective shadow that kept her view unobstructed. She missed Pup's first command and wondered which language he used to communicate with the K9. English was fine, but many handlers preferred other languages—like German—to prevent confusion during missions, since dogs trained in a different tongue wouldn't be thrown off by anyone else's commands in English.

That kind of mix-up could spell disaster.

Her gaze flicked to Daylan, realizing she hadn't heard his commands either. She turned to him, her eyes briefly locking with his before returning to the course. "What languages do you use for commands?"

"English, German, French, and Deutsch."

Elena did a double-take. She whistled softly. "That's impressive." She'd only worked in English and German with Tiki. Clearly, she had room to upgrade her training.

"Thanks." Daylan couldn't hide the hint of pride in his voice.

When Casey eagerly bounded through the tunnel, Elena turned to Daylan with curiosity. "Why did Buddy hesitate at the tunnel?"

Daylan shuffled his feet, glancing away. "I hoped you didn't notice that."

Elena chuckled softly and turned back to the course, catching Casey clear a challenging four-foot wall. "That's my job—to notice everything."

"Honestly, I'm not completely sure. We haven't trained much with tunnels, and he's obviously not a fan of them."

Elena's brow furrowed in thought. "That's not ideal." She watched Pup and Casey cross the finish line, their times faster than Daylan and Buddy's. But she reminded herself—they'd run this course before.

"I'll work on it."

A proud Pup and Casey approached, with Casey already chomping on her loud, squeaky toy.

Elena turned her gaze to Daylan. "No. We'll work on it together."

She turned back to Pup. "Great job."

A proud gleam in his eyes said he was soaking up the praise.

"Thanks." He tilted his head toward Daylan. "Any questions?"

Daylan crossed his arms, a skeptical arch to his brow. "Just one. How many times have you practiced?"

Pup shrugged, a cheeky grin on his face. "Not enough. Never enough."

Elena appreciated that fiery drive. Practice makes perfect, after all. "Gentlemen, none of this competitiveness. We're a team."

Pup's shoulders sagged a bit as he glanced at Elena, his voice playful. "It's just friendly competition."

Elena shot a quick look at Daylan, who kept his arms crossed, a hint of a smirk on his face. "Sure, just friendly."

She wanted to shake some sense into them, knowing that beneath their banter lay a simmering storm that could explode at any moment. She took a deep breath. "Okay. Let's drop it."

She knew this tension would flare again once she began timing their course, and she inwardly groaned at the thought, because she was preparing for the next round of challenges ahead.

"What about your dog?" A sparkle of curiosity lit Daylan's eyes. "Can she run the course with only three legs?"

Elena's stomach clenched at the handler's words, but she quickly steadied herself. Tiki was in perfect health. She hadn't yet tried this course, but Elena had no doubt she could handle it. Well, except for the high jumps. They'd be a strain on her joints that Elena would not allow. Maybe Tiki wasn't as fast as Casey, but she'd give Buddy a run for his money.

Instead of snapping at Daylan for pointing out the obvious, Elena offered a confident, radiant smile. "Even though she's no longer an 'attack' dog, we'll give it a try." She knelt beside Tiki. "What do you say, girl? Ready for some fun?"

Tiki barked eagerly, her tail wagging furiously, as if she knew she was about to prove everyone's doubts wrong.

Elena's heart swelled. Her K9 had always been more than a K9 partner. She was family, a loyal partner in every sense.

For a moment, Elena hesitated. Should she leave these two men alone? Then she almost laughed at herself. They were grown men, not boys looking for a locker-room brawl. Whatever rivalry simmered between them, it would be settled on the course.

As she and Tiki moved toward the starting line, Elena leaned in close. "You know, girl, these men might be more of a challenge than I thought. I hope we've made the right choice." Her voice was a mix of determination and a touch of nervousness. She had handled plenty of egos during her SWAT days, but this was uncharted territory—balancing her confidence with new challenges, all while trying to keep everyone's pride intact.

Even after losing her leg, Tiki's resilience shone brightly. Elena had been bringing her to the police K9 obstacle course regularly, even before her retirement. Tiki had always been a star—sometimes the lead, sometimes the hero. Now, even with her limitations, she still faced each challenge with unwavering determination.

Standing at the starting line, Elena took a deep breath, heart pounding with anticipation. "We can do this." A surge of hope sprang up inside her.

She grabbed her smartwatch, eager to see how they'd fare. "Ready, girl?" Pressing the start button, then began. "Tiki, aus!" They sprinted toward the first obstacle —a small jump that she knew Tiki could manage without discomfort. "Hopp."

Tiki's agility was incredible. She expertly sailed over the jump, her tail high with pride. They moved swiftly to the next challenge—a narrow beam, which Tiki crossed confidently. Despite the hurdles, she met each one head-on, unshaken and full of dogged resolve.

She led Tiki past the open doorway, despite Tiki whining her displeasure. "I know, girl." She had no doubt Tiki would master it if given the chance, but the strain wasn't worth it.

At the finish line, Elena paused, overwhelmed with pride. She praised Tiki enthusiastically, forgetting about the stopwatch. As she clicked stop, she grimaced, realizing that, even with their best effort, their time was slower than when Tiki had run the course as a police dog. But in her heart, she knew this wasn't about speed. It was about their unbreakable spirit and the incredible bond they shared.

And proudly demonstrated to her new subordinates that they could work together as a team.

The men clapped half-heartedly as she approached, their muted applause making her wonder what secrets they had been whispering about while she and Tiki had made the run. She shook her head, scolding herself. She couldn't afford to worry about things beyond her control.

Tiki plopped down, playfully tugging at the stuffed toy Elena had pulled from her back pocket, her tail wagging with pure joy.

"Good job." Daylan's genuine surprise showed on his face. "Much better than I expected."

Elena hesitated, unsure if it was a compliment or a slight. Still, she managed a small smile. "Thanks."

"Yeah, great job." Pup grinned. "I can see why you want to keep her in service."

She startled at the compliment, caught off guard by the warmth in his tone. Considering their strained relationship, she hadn't expected something so kind from him.

Feeling invigorated, Elena squared her shoulders as she faced the handlers. "Now that I've seen you in action on the course, we're moving to the other training facilities. Next, we'll—"

Before she could finish, Pup's voice cut in sharply. "Search for drugs?"

Elena's stomach tightened. She could've melted into the green grass. He was never going to let that go—hell, she wasn't either. She'd left the damn force, so why was everyone still so eager to make her life miserable? Or was it the same person who blew up Mark's home? A chill ran down her spine at the thought of whether Mark or she was the intended target. Or, maybe both of them.

Daylan looked between them. "Search for drugs?"

"Yeah." Pup's grin broadened. "Let's see how they do searching for drugs."

Right then, she'd never wanted to smack a man before, but Pup's relentless innocence was pushing her to her limits. How could someone so kind-hearted to his dog, who wore black like a badass and sported a panty-dropping smile, be such an infuriating pain in her ass?

Despite herself, she couldn't help but frown at the thought—and the undeniable chemistry simmering beneath it.

Chapter Ten

Elena's day had taken a nosedive from bad to catastrophic. It started with the chaos of the drug search setup, and then Pup wanting to talk—hell, she'd asked him to commit a crime, and he'd gone through with it. To make things worse, he had been insistent that the dogs search for drugs, as if taunting her.

Had he really asked if the drugs were hers? The question hit her hard. She couldn't believe anyone would think that of her. Yet, somehow, she knew he saw her as nothing more than a bitchy woman standing in his way.

She refused to chalk any of this up to his age because anyone would think the same, given her behavior. So, she had to stop using age as a reason. Why she was fixated on it, she wasn't sure. It kept nagging at her—not because he was younger, but because she was older.

Tiki whined softly on her bed near the couch, seeking Elena's attention.

"Come on up, girl." Elena patted the worn fabric of the couch. As she looked at it, she wondered how her life had traveled so far downhill. She'd never been wealthy, working as a public servant, but she'd had good things—

things she once cherished.

She sighed deeply. Things were just things. What she truly needed were better memories to drown out the wreckage of her life.

Her only bright spot had been her job with HIS. But now, with Pup's antics running wild, she questioned if she could keep that lifeline afloat.

"Enough of this melancholy."

The sudden ring of her phone sent a jolt through her, her heart pounding in the stillness of the night. Who could be calling at such an hour? Panic surged as she imagined the worst—a family emergency. With trembling hands, she snatched her phone from the side table, her eyes widening at the detective's number flashing on the screen. Answering with a mix of fear and anticipation, she braced herself for whatever news of the explosion investigation awaited. Had they uncovered something new about her stalker, or was she about to be thrust back into the spotlight as a potential suspect?

"Hello?"

"Miss Raymundo, this is Detective Booker."

She despised being called Miss Raymundo, having always been known as Elena on the force. "Yes, William?" She deliberately made it personal. "Any breakthroughs in the case?"

A huff echoed through the line, likely from her using his first name, but she didn't mind. Keeping it casual was key to keeping his focus on the case. After all, it was Mark's house, but the police suspected she was the one who had amassed dangerous enemies. And they wouldn't be far off.

"We've arrested Mark Thompson for the bombing. I just wanted to let you know."

"Wait, what?" Had he just said what she thought? "But, that's his house. He could've been there when it happened. He almost was."

"But you said he checked his watch before leaving the scene swiftly."

Elena shook her head, her voice firm. "So? We were arguing, and he was asked to leave. He did. End of story." It was surprising even to her that she found herself defending Mark, but she was certain he couldn't have been behind it. He was nearly home when the explosion occurred. A shiver ran down her spine as she recalled how narrowly she had escaped the blast.

"I can't go into the details, but trust us, it's him. I thought you should know so you can close the case in your mind."

No way in hell would she close the case in her mind. Mark couldn't have done it. He was a grade-A asshole, but not an explosives expert. "And…why did he do it?"

"The money. Now, that's all I'm going to say on the matter." Detective Booker disconnected the call.

Elena couldn't believe it. None of it. Mark? Not her stalker? What had become of her stalker? She hadn't sensed his presence lately—the lingering feeling of being watched had faded. Could it be that he'd finally left her alone? Perhaps she was finally safe, or maybe luck was on her side, and he was behind bars for some other crime, leaving her in peace.

She longed for a good run with Tiki, but at this hour —what was it, nearly ten?—she knew it wasn't the best idea. "We'd best try to get some sleep." She gently petted Tiki, whose head rested on her lap. "But I can't sleep. My mind won't stop." Elena looked down at the dog, whose eyes had already closed, and a small smile tugged at her lips. "At least one of us can sleep."

She cleared her mind of the call, but then Pup lingered in her thoughts. She wanted to give him a swift kick in the ass to calm his attitude, but that wasn't an option now. She knew she had to be the bigger person— to figure out how to mend their fractured working relationship, even if they didn't see eye to eye off the field.

She reminded herself they lived in the same building. She'd probably be invited over to Pup's place by one of the agents, perhaps even against Pup's wishes. How should she handle that? Craving camaraderie, yes, but at what cost to the fragile truce she hoped to build with Pup?

Her mind spun in chaotic circles as the night pressed heavily with unspoken questions and tentative hopes, questioning her sanity at every turn. Why was Pup occupying so much of her thoughts when she had real work to focus on? She caught herself thinking about the agent again. Yes, he was undeniably attractive, but was she truly attracted to him? Or was she just fooling herself? Deep down, she knew the answer. It was the latter, and that made her fight those feelings all the more. She was his boss, and he was young—at least in years, if not in maturity. She'd thought wrongly about his maturity when he hadn't deserved it. That needed to stop.

A groan escaped her lips, and she cursed sharply in Spanish, tired of the mental tug-of-war. Enough. Focus.

"So." She bit her lip. "Who wants me in jail—or worse?" She knew the harsh truth that law enforcement didn't fare well behind bars. Not because of the bars themselves, but because someone on the inside wanted to see them dead, and escape was only a pipe dream.

Running through the list of police officers and criminals who might want to see her pay was overwhelming. She couldn't believe malice could motivate so many, but her trust in others was faltering. She no longer believed a criminal she arrested would forgive her, nor did she trust her fellow officers blindly.

"But who would want this?" A shiver ran down her spine. It couldn't be Mark. He hadn't known of her breakup before it happened. Heck, she'd barely known.

The silence in her life had been broken. She knew vigilance was her only safeguard, and she would remain alert, eyes constantly scanning for danger.

That was why she had to ensure her neighbors didn't just allow anyone into the building, like she suspected Pup might. Guilt gnawed at her for once again imagining the worst about the agent, but exhaustion pressed down on her eyelids. It was time to sleep, and she'd figure everything out in the morning.

"Let's get to bed, girl." She gently slid Tiki's head off her lap. She stood, stretching her arms above her head, feeling the satisfying relief as her tense muscles loosened.

Suddenly, a loud thump echoed from next door, making her heart skip a beat. What the hell?

She turned to Tiki, whose ears were perked, eyes fixed on the wall separating her apartment from Pup's. At first, she thought it was her stalker, but then she realized the sound came from Pup's apartment. Another thump followed, and concern for Pup crept in.

Should she investigate or stay out of his business? But what if someone was breaking in? The noise sounded too deliberate to ignore.

Her fear of the agent pushed her forward despite her instinct to stay safe. She quietly moved to the safe in her bedroom, grabbing her Kimber 9mm. It was a petite gun —smaller than most—but it fit her small hand perfectly, and right now, it felt like her only protection.

She hadn't planned to bring Tiki, but the K9 was alert and by her side. The dog had an odd ability to sense danger, and she wondered how she had ever trained that into her. Still, now wasn't the time to think about it. The dog wanted to go, and she wasn't afraid to let Tiki lead since she obeyed her commands.

With her hand resting on her apartment doorknob, she paused, glancing back at Tiki with a mix of regret and resolve.

Letting the dog go first had cost Tiki a leg. What would it cost her this time? She couldn't attack any longer. Or, at least, she shouldn't. A flicker of doubt crossed her mind, questioning whether continuing was worth the risk. Her heart pounded fiercely as she hesitated, caught between instinct and caution.

Elena's eyes fluttered shut as she wrestled with her desire to save Pup, but the sound of another loud thump and a strained groan cut through the silence, pushing her to a decision.

"Bleib, Tiki." When she spoke German, Tiki understood she meant serious business, and the dog obediently plopped her butt on the ground, whining softly.

She believed she could handle this on her own.

Carefully, she exited her apartment, moving with cautious intent down the short hallway, ears straining and eyes scanning the surroundings. Everything looked normal—at least, it appeared so, though she'd only just moved in and hadn't had time to grasp the full picture.

Her gaze fell on the front door, which was propped open. A surge of anger flared. If Pup were responsible, he'd pay dearly, especially after she had come to save his life.

With silent precision, Elena removed the brick blocking the door and gently eased it shut. The latch clicked softly—a sound magnified in the tense silence, like a shotgun blast. Yet, despite the sharp noise, the air remained eerily still, holding its breath.

Gliding toward Pup's door, Elena noticed it wasn't quite shut. Either the criminal intruder hadn't bothered to push it closed behind him or her, or Pup hadn't. Either way, it was her lucky break. She didn't have to wrestle with a locked door. As she reached out to grasp the knob, a sudden sound froze her in place. Really? Was that the problem?

"Oh, Kevin." The female voice was tinged with annoyance. "Why are you drunk? And during the workweek?"

Kevin? Elena's mind raced. Who the hell was inside? Realizing she was about to become an uninvited guest, she instinctively turned to back away.

Suddenly, Pup's voice, slurred and thick, called out,

"You forgot to close the door," as it grew louder, signaling his approach.

With nowhere to hide, Elena pressed her back against the outside of the door, holding her breath, praying he wouldn't glance into the hallway and see her lurking nearby.

With her heart pounding loudly in her ears, Elena barely registered the door closing and the soft click of the lock being bolted.

She let out a shaky sigh, relief flooding her as she glimpsed her narrow escape from the unwelcome encounter with Pup and his drunken state—and the woman he had with him.

Was she just a hookup? Or a regular?

As self-criticism gnawed at her, Elena slowly slid away from the wall, her footsteps whisper-quiet as she made her way back to her apartment. Once inside, she closed and bolted the door behind her, heart still racing.

She turned toward Tiki, who sat loyal and unmoved. "Tiki, hier."

The dog leapt up instantly, bounding over to her with concern in her eyes, barking lightly as if to reassure her she was safe now.

"Hush, girl." Elena gently petted Tiki. With a deep breath, she headed to her bedroom to store the weapon securely in her specially designated safe. Suddenly, a sharp knock echoed through her apartment, making her jump before she could press her thumb to the scanner.

Her body stiffened. Who could possibly be visiting her at this late hour?

A cold rush of fear gripped her, like a serpent

slithering through her veins. Her mind raced—had her stalker sneaked into the building while the door had been ajar? But would he really knock if that were the case?

Then, a familiar voice shattered the silence. "Elena, open this door!" Pup's commanding voice boomed as he knocked again.

Instinct taking over, Elena forced herself to breathe evenly. She set the weapon down, but her resolve hardened. She moved back to the living room, her heart pounding, and prepared to face the drunk on the other side.

Unlocking the door quickly, she yanked it open and shot a sharp glare at Pup, who, despite the drunkenness, looked surprisingly unbothered—dazed, yes, but still charmingly disheveled. Her instincts flickered. She shook her head in frustration. "What do you want at this hour?" Her tone was sharp with a mix of sternness and annoyance.

"Keep the noise down." He'd slurred and shot her a lazy grin. "Some of us are trying to sleep."

She rolled her eyes, scoffing. "Is that what they call it?" His balance faltered, and she almost reached out to steady him. "You're drunk."

He nodded, unapologetic. "Yep." His gaze drifted into her apartment, and she stepped into the hallway, shutting the door behind her, leaving Tiki whining at the noise.

"Sorry about Tiki. She thought she heard a noise." Her voice softened just a tad, though the unspoken suspicion hung in the air.

"Just keep it down. The neighbors don't like it."

Before she could even respond, that melodic voice caught her attention again. "Kevin, come back. It's too late to bother the neighbors."

Elena cocked her head, a mischievous smile playing on her lips. "Yeah, Kevin. It's way too late to bother the neighbors—especially when you've got company."

Her ears picked up a hint of jealousy in her tone, and she secretly hoped the drunken "Kevin" didn't catch it.

He looked her over as he swayed, dismissing her with a shrug. "Whatever." He turned toward his apartment. "I'm coming, Maria."

The name sent a ripple through Elena's mind—another Latina in Pup's life? She reminded herself that she was his boss, that she'd focus on building her relationship with Pup first, and then, maybe, figure out the rest. But deep down, the thought of "Maria"—only part of Pup's world—bothered her more than she liked to admit.

Chapter Eleven

Pup groggily woke up, feeling like the world had gone mad. A pounding in his head and a dry mouth confirmed his wild night—the result of too many drinks. Thank goodness his sister Maria had been there when he called, ready to pick him up since he hadn't planned on getting drunk or having a designated driver.

He cursed himself, rolling over and pulling the pillow over his ears to block out the relentless noise outside his apartment. When did construction crews start working at the crack of dawn?

Startled, he reached for his phone on the side table to check the time.

"Oh shit." He leaped out of bed only to stumble and teeter back, off balance from the sudden rush of alertness.

Sitting on the edge of his bed, he wiped his tired face, already feeling the weight of the day ahead. Pup looked up with alert eyes as Casey whined softly from the corner, curled up on the bed.

"Sorry, girl, no playtime this morning. We're already running late for work."

But Casey's needs always came first.

Pup yanked on a pair of jeans and a sweatshirt, grabbed Casey's leash, and stepped outside. As he froze his ass off, allowing Casey to do her business, he hurried back into his apartment. A quick shower, hastily dressed —there was no time for shaving or grooming. He had to go as he was.

Tossing down the aspirin and grabbing a bottle of water, Pup snatched his keys and burst out of the building, curiosity piqued about who might have left the door ajar once again. Seeing the parking lot empty and silent, he swiftly removed the brick from the doorway and rushed toward his vehicle, heart pounding with anticipation.

When he reached his truck, the clock was already ticking. An hour behind schedule, with a forty-minute drive ahead—assuming no traffic. He buckled Casey into her seat, then moved to the driver's seat. He cursed softly as he started the vehicle. The engine came alive, only to blast him with frigid air as it warmed up.

Rubbing his hands together, he turned on the steering wheel heater and shifted into gear. No use dwelling on it —he was late, and the day wasn't going to wait. As he merged into traffic, he gritted his teeth, resigned but trying not to lose his temper.

What was waiting for him today? The Hamilton brothers never set strict arrival times for their team unless there was a briefing, so he figured he'd be okay. But then, a reminder hit him—Elena had scheduled time with the handlers at seven a.m.

He slammed his hand against the steering wheel. "Great. Just what I needed." Now, he'd have to see what kind of boss Elena really was.

Fifty minutes later, he slammed the brakes into a parking spot at HIS headquarters, heart pounding with urgency. He shot a glance around—no one in sight. Relief washed over him as he exhaled deeply. He opened the door, released Casey, and decided against using her leash.

"Casey, Geh Voraus." The dog darted ahead with unrestrained energy. She hadn't had park time this morning, and Pup wanted her to burn off steam before the training began. He checked his watch—an hour ago.

Hustling toward the kennel where they were supposed to meet, he was met with an empty building and the surrounding area. He'd missed them. They might be at the obstacle course or inside one of the training buildings, hunting for drugs, people, or hidden items. Who knew what plans had been set in motion?

Suddenly, a voice broke through the quiet, startling him. "Lost?"

It was Devon—computer whiz, former CIA agent, and the family's sharpest mind.

Embarrassment flushed his face. "I'm late."

Devon glanced at his watch, then crossed his arms, giving him that skeptical look. "No shit."

He'd never been scolded by a Hamilton brother before, but he felt that record was about to change.

"Speaking of shit, you look like it. What happened?"

Pup startled. He'd thought he'd done a decent job hiding his hangover, but now he remembered not shaving or styling his hair—great. He inwardly groaned.

"Nothing to worry about."

Devon raised an eyebrow, clearly not convinced. "When it hits HIS, it does. Now spill. What's going on?"

Pup shrugged, trying to play it off. "Just drinking a bit too much last night." It wasn't against the rules to unwind after hours, but it had affected work this time.

Devon leaned against the kennel wall, his gaze steady. "That's not like you, Pup. You're the responsible one. What's going on?"

Pup's stomach clenched. Really? They'd trusted him, counted on him. Then why wasn't he in the lead handler position? He shook off the thought—no point dwelling.

"Sorry, Devon."

"Don't just apologize to me. You'd better talk to Elena and Daylan. They're waiting for you and a briefing." Devon's voice held a hint of concern.

Pup straightened, energy crackling through him like static. Today might be the day—finally, Casey would get her chance to prove herself to the organization. "At HQ?" His voice was tinged with anticipation as he referred to the one building where all classified briefings took place.

Devon nodded, pushing off the wall with purpose. "Let's go." His footsteps echoed softly as he walked ahead, Pup at his heels.

"Casey, fuss." Today was possibly her first real op. Pup made a mental note to keep his focus. He'd keep commands in German to ensure Casey stayed on track.

The K9 dashed over and fell into step beside him, her paws clicking softly against the pavement as they approached the familiar, windowless building.

Pup's excitement buzzed louder than the churning in his gut. His stomach was no longer sour. It was alive, eager for action.

Devon keyed in his code, and the door swung open into a spacious entry hall. Ahead, a second door— recently added for lockdown—stood as a new obstacle Pup couldn't quite understand. The building was already secure with just the one door, after all.

He shrugged internally. There must be a reason, even if he couldn't see it. After all, he wasn't being paid the big bucks for security upgrades.

When they reached the bustling operations briefing room, Pup's eyes immediately locked onto Elena. She was huddled with Jesse and Daylan, speaking in hushed, urgent tones. As Elena nodded and turned to Daylan, extending her hand, Pup's curiosity skyrocketed. What could be going on?

Daylan shook hands with Elena and then headed towards Pup, his expression serious.

Pup slowed his step, feeling the weight of anticipation.

"Good luck." Daylan passed by with a determined look before heading for the exit.

Pup hesitated, then cleared his throat. "Okay." He stretched the word as his gaze returned to Elena, who was now listening intently to Jesse.

Realizing he had come to a halt, Pup took a step forward, Casey at his side. "Sorry I'm late." He tried to sound casual but aware of the room's attention. Unfortunately, everyone looked his way, and Pup's face flushed with embarrassment. He hadn't intended to draw such notice, but his words had carried farther than expected.

Elena snapped her gaze to his, and her eyes

narrowed, sharp as a predator assessing its prey.

Uh-oh. She was pissed—rightfully so, after he was late and knocked on her door last night like some kind of trespasser.

He hadn't exactly had a plan—just the excuse of Tiki barking—to justify his late-night check-in, but he had heard someone lurking outside his apartment, and flashbacks of the cop's "stalker" comment flooded his mind.

Pup saw Jesse cross his arms in his peripheral vision, eyebrows raised in concern and suspicion. "Everything okay, Pup?"

His gaze still locked with Elena's, he gave a subtle nod. "Sure thing, boss."

Elena broke eye contact, glancing at her watch with a calculated nonchalance before locking eyes with him again.

"Glad you could finally join us." Her voice dripped with mockery about his tardiness.

Realizing there was no winning this moment, he grinned, choosing to double down on his carefree attitude and ride it out. "So am I."

Breaking the tense silence, Devon suddenly cleared his throat with a sharp sound. "Let's get to it, shall we?"

Pup nodded eagerly, approaching the mission brief table with purpose.

Casey, instinctively at his heels, followed without hesitation. She'd often been here when they worked as a team, but this time felt different—more critical.

Pup sensed the change, and excitement flickered in his eyes.

Devon determinedly pressed a hidden key to activate the embedded computer. The screen flickered to life before them, casting an eerie glow across the room.

Pup's eyes widened in disbelief. Why was Devon showing them a picture of a pop star? Had he somehow accessed his personal computer instead of his work one?

Jesse caught Pup's attention with a spark in his eyes. "Meet Zee Alvarez. She's one of the hottest rising stars in the music scene today."

That wasn't exactly news to Pup or anyone who tuned into the radio. Her soulful songs about lost loves played on repeat, stirring emotions in listeners whether they wanted to feel them or not.

"We've been hired by her." Devon's voice had a hint of excitement.

Pup scanned the room, noticing everyone was back to their own business, barely giving the briefing a second thought. "Which team is on point?" He wondered why only he and Elena were called in instead of an entire team.

Jesse and Devon exchanged glances. Jesse nodded toward him and Elena. "You two are it."

A surge of disbelief and satisfaction washed over Pup. Disbelief—it was only two handlers and their dogs working with a star of Zee's caliber. Satisfaction—that Casey would be going on this adventure alongside him.

"I'm sorry." Elena's voice was sharp with urgency. "You mean just Pup, me, and who else?"

"Your K9s." Devon's confident smirk played on his lips, as if it were the most obvious thing in the world.

To Pup, it seemed obvious, too. He'd been through enough briefings with the brothers to know how they tagged certain things.

Pup was ready for more information. "What exactly are we doing? Doesn't she have a security detail? Or is HIS taking over?"

Devon pressed a button, and suddenly, a series of handwritten notes flashed before their eyes, each one more alarming than the last. The exact words were highlighted, raising Pup's brow in concern. "I'll blow you sky-high."

Jesse, sitting across the massive table, leaned forward, eyes intense. "She's been receiving threats. She increased her security team, but they're worried about bombs. Her team doesn't have the assets for that kind of mission."

Pup's anticipation grew. "So, she wants us to sweep her hotel room and venue while she's here." The star was scheduled to perform in Baltimore soon, but he hadn't kept track of the dates because he hadn't planned to go.

"Yes, and no." Devon nodded grimly, then typed rapidly. A detailed performance schedule for Zee emerged. "You and your K9s are heading on the road with her and her team."

Elena gasped, her eyes widening in shock. "You can't be serious. Both of us traveling together?"

Pup straightened, his gaze locking onto her. "And why not? What's wrong with that?"

Elena backpedaled, her voice trembling. "I didn't mean it like that, I swear."

He almost yelled, "The hell you didn't!" but caught himself, tightening his jaw.

"It's just—why both of us? Wouldn't one team

suffice?"

Pup relaxed, a slow smile spreading across his face. "That makes a lot of sense." He turned to Jesse and Devon, nodding firmly. "She's got a valid point." The tension eased slightly as the idea sank in.

"Simple. It's Casey's first mission, so I'd like backup." Jesse's eyes sparkled with quiet pride as he spoke.

Pup was tempted to boast that Casey had been chosen over Elena and Daylan's K9s, but held back, knowing timing was everything.

Devon cleared his throat, breaking the moment. "And, Elena and Tiki can still teach her on the road."

Elena glanced at Pup, concern flickering in her eyes. "What if you need a team in our absence?"

Pup nodded in agreement, understanding the gravity of the question.

Jesse shrugged, a relaxed smile on his face. "We'll handle that hurdle if it occurs." Then, with a quick motion, he stood. "You leave in the morning to join her and her team in Sacramento." He paused, eyes twinkling with mischief. "And, Pup, try to shave while you're with them." A grin spread across his lips.

Pup tried to hide his amusement with a subtle chuckle, then forced a grin. "Sure thing, boss." He didn't mind Jesse calling him out on his appearance. Most men didn't usually keep it high and tight—shaving and grooming—while between ops, and the brothers allowed it. But when on an operation, agents had to adapt. If that meant shaving every day, so be it.

He turned to Elena with a quick nod. "Ready, boss?"

She shot him a tired look, her eyes narrowing slightly. "Sure thing."

Why was she so worried about traveling with him? He was just a schoolboy compared to what he'd heard about SWAT officers in the field. She'd soon see what a handful he could be, and he'd make up for all the wrongs he'd done—including that midnight intrusion.

That reminded him—who had been lurking outside his door late at night?

As the room buzzed with anticipation and camaraderie, and plans were set into motion, each person quietly committed to their part in what was sure to be an unforgettable mission, Pup wondered if this op would finally break the barrier between them or build upon it.

Chapter Twelve

Elena let out a sharp string of Spanish curses as she hurriedly packed her suitcase. Anger flickered in her eyes. Did HIS really think she couldn't handle this on her own, or trust her and Tiki to do the job? Just because Tiki had one limitation didn't mean she needed help.

Elena didn't need to train Casey for the field on the trip. Sure, there was time, but still.... She resented having Pup tagging along like a constant shadow.

Frustration boiling over, she tossed a pair of navy blue slacks and a crisp white shirt into the suitcase. Would they even expect her to wear suits? She scoffed at the idea. She didn't own a business suit, but she had some nice blouses that would do.

Grabbing an old pair of low, navy heels, she slipped them into the suitcase, then sighed as she sank onto the bed, her mind racing with everything that had occurred.

Since Zee's head of security wanted to brief them personally and refused to leave his boss's side, Elena and Pup barely had time to plan. And they had no idea how long their assignment would last while traveling with a singer. It made Elena want to scream. Did they even have groupies, drugs, and all the things she despised? This was going to be one hell of an assignment. And then, toss in Pup as her partner—well, that was enough to give her a major headache.

She looked at Tiki, curled up in her bed in the corner of the room. "Until further notice, we're on detail with Zee Alvarez."

How do you even prepare for something like that? How much luggage is too much, and what won't survive the long travels?

At least she didn't have children or a spouse waiting at home.

Or did Pup? She thought about the woman who was with Pup last night. Her stomach soured at that thought—maybe Pup had someone close, someone waiting for him —and that bitter suspicion only fueled her rising anger.

What did she care if he had someone to love? Just because her love life was a mess didn't mean others couldn't have one.

But Pup—that little spark of defiance flared up inside her. She shot up from the bed and let out a curse. Maldita sea! Why should she care?

She knew she should check if he had a spouse, given her supervisory role. She'd need to ensure the woman was cared for if Pup was dispatched on a long assignment, like he would be starting tomorrow. But then again, she wasn't his direct supervisor. She only needed to know how well he handled his K9 partner. Still, the curiosity gnawed at her, refusing to let go.

A sudden knock at her door jolted her, her heart pounding as she listened to the sound. She wasn't expecting anyone, so instinct took over. She quickly moved to her safe, retrieving her 9mm. It wasn't that she thought an axe murderer would be lurking, though, considering someone had been stalking her, may have tried to blow her up, and set her up with drugs, caution was essential.

"Who is it?" Standing on her tiptoes to peer through the peephole, she only stumbled and fell flat on her feet. Pup was standing there. Why now?

Her mind raced. Only one way to find out. She tucked the gun into her waistband and, heart fluttering like a butterfly, she opened the door slightly. Then, she pasted a smile on her face. "What are you doing here?"

Pup raised an eyebrow, probably at how sharply that welcome sounded.

She cleared her throat, trying to regain her composure. "Sorry. What can I do for you?"

His dazzling smile almost made her forget her surroundings.

Wait—what? No way. Well, yes, but no way— especially if they were to hit the road together. That would be a disaster waiting to happen.

"You can let me in, for starters."

"Why?" Elena narrowed her eyes at him, a flicker of curiosity and wariness crossing her face. That familiar, mischievous smile he often wore appeared again, sending a strange flutter through her stomach. Maldita sea! She scolded herself internally. She couldn't afford to think of him that way. Romantic notions and forbidden sparks never ended well, especially when it was between a supervisor and a subordinate.

He spread his arms wide, a casual gesture that somehow felt like an invitation and a warning all at once. "We need to talk."

Elena hesitated, knowing she owed him an explanation about the drug setup, although she doubted she had enough information to satisfy him. Not that she was eager to share. After all, he was her subordinate. Still, she nodded, resigned. "Okay."

She pushed open the door, stepped aside, and motioned for him to enter. A part of her instinctively knew this was probably a mistake, but curiosity and nerves compelled her to proceed.

Pup stalked into her apartment, his eyes sweeping the space with a knowing look. He looked around, nodding slowly as if confirming something unseen.

Elena wasn't sure what he was acknowledging—her sparse, bare-bones space already lacked artwork or enough furniture to fill the silence.

In the living room, Pup paused, then turned suddenly, and Elena nearly collided with him.

She instinctively stepped back, creating space between them. The closeness was unsettling, too intimate for her comfort. Heart pounding, she glanced up, voice steady but cautious. "What?"

He intensely scrutinized her, leaving her feeling exposed and almost raw. His eyes held hers momentarily, and her vulnerability was virtually palpable. Then, he shook his head and turned away, dismissing whatever he saw. "Nothing." He strolled to the couch and settled down as if he'd been invited.

Pup raised an eyebrow. "Did you know that the

Basenji is known as the 'barkless dog' because it makes yodel-like sounds?"

Elena clenched her jaw, the delicate, almost sensual vulnerability evaporating, replaced by a spark of irritation. She did know that, but his attempt to make himself comfortable hit a nerve. "Have a seat." She settled into a matching armchair.

Pup leaned back on the couch, resting an arm casually over the backrest and crossing one leg over the other thigh. He raised an eyebrow, a mischievous glint in his eyes. "Well?"

Nervously—she hated feeling this way—she bit her lip, hesitating. He could be alluding to so many things, so she decided to keep him guessing, acting as if she had no clue what he was talking about. "Well, what?"

He shook his head, a scoff escaping his lips. "Are you kidding me? You had drugs in your vehicle, and you had me flush them down the toilet so the cops,"—he narrowed his eyes—"that I'm guessing you know were coming didn't find them. That 'what.'"

A heavy stone settled in her stomach. Earlier, he'd asked if the drugs were hers. Did he even believe her? It wasn't much, and it didn't clear her name, but for some reason, his opinion—that little flicker of doubt—mattered more than she wanted to admit.

There was no reason not to share what she'd told Jesse and Devon this morning. Eventually, it would reach him. So why hold back?

"Yesterday, I got a call from a friend—" she began, but before she could finish, she raised a hand to stop him from speaking.

"Let me finish. A friend, who wishes to stay anonymous, called to warn me about drugs hidden in my vehicle, and there was even a dispatch alert about it." She shifted uncomfortably in her seat, feeling exposed. "And, well—you know the rest."

Pup sat still, studying her intently. He shifted his position when he spoke, uncrossing his legs and leaning forward with his forearms resting on his thighs. "That's not much of a story. I already figured all that out myself."

"But—" She was about to remind him that he'd thought the drugs might be hers, but cut herself off.

He leaned back, shrugging. "Honestly, I still have doubts. But if Jesse believes you, then I do too. You'll learn that HIS isn't like that shit SWAT team. We're a real team...a family."

She craved a family environment so fiercely that she could almost taste the longing. The first colleague she'd met had been Pup, and let's just say, things had gone south faster than she could load her pistol magazine. "Okay." Honestly, she had no idea what else to say. She knew she should apologize for being such a bitch to him, but the words stuck in her throat.

Before she could second-guess herself, Pup pushed to his feet. "All right then. How much are you packing?"

She stood, brushing past him and heading toward the door. "Enough that I'll do laundry on the road often."

He exited and turned back with a grin. "Sounds like a plan." Then, to her surprise, he extended his hand. "How about we try a mulligan?"

Confused but curious, she nodded. "Okay, I don't know what that means, but sure."

He introduced himself with a playful nod. "Hi, I'm Pup." Then he looked at her expectantly. "Now, you introduce yourself and shake my hand."

Lightbulb moments flashed in her mind. She finally got what a mulligan was. A smile broke across her face. "Hi, I'm Elena. Nice to meet you."

Could it really be that simple to start mending their fractured relationship? She hoped so, though doubt still lingered.

"I'll see you in the morning." He turned toward his apartment.

Elena started to suggest they ride together, but decided they hadn't yet reached that level of comfort, so she just nodded. "In the morning."

Elena closed the door behind Pup with a heavy sigh, hoping that things might finally settle down. With their professional duties now taking precedence, perhaps their trivial arguments would fade into the background. Or so she hoped.

After tucking her gun away, she turned her attention to her suitcase, determined to pack more efficiently. Just as she was about to dive into the task, her phone rang, offering a much-needed distraction.

Her face lit up when she saw Luis's name on the screen. "Hola, Luis," she greeted with a smile. But her joy was short-lived as Luis's words hit her like a cold wave.

"Mark's been released, and he's blaming you for having him arrested."

Chapter Thirteen

Pup couldn't believe his eyes. He was on a private jet for the flight from Baltimore to Sacramento. Sure, he'd flown in private jets before, during some of HIS operations, but this one was unlike any other. Its shimmering surfaces and gaudy decor made it quite unique. Yep, it was downright over-the-top.

He stifled a chuckle at the burst of orange and purple swirls, checks, and circles that adorned the jet's interior. It felt like a blast from the 60s, or at least what he imagined that era to be.

Wanting to get Elena's take on the decor, he glanced in her direction. She drifted off before they finished the takeoff roll and was still asleep. However, he had a sneaking suspicion she had been awake for a while, feigning sleep. He didn't understand why and decided not to call her out. He'd remember the slight.

Reclining comfortably, he nestled a pillow behind his head and gazed at the plane's ceiling. It was painted with wavy lines that made him almost woozy. He hoped the entire trip wasn't like this plane—nauseating.

With Casey curled up in the seat next to him, Pup

closed his eyes, lost in thought about the evening before. He and Elena had reached a fragile truce, and he was determined to honor his part. Yet, her feigned sleep to avoid conversation spoke volumes about how she might handle their new beginning.

Trying to brush off the sting, Pup reminded himself she was just a colleague. But as he slowly peeked at her sleeping form, he saw there was far more to her than just another agent. An unmistakable curiosity ignited within him, and he was eager to learn everything about her.

Tiki looked at him, resting over Elena, and Pup realized that at some point, his perception shifted from seeing her as a bitch to simply considering her...intriguing.

Charles, the flight attendant, glided past and, spotting Pup awake, gently knelt beside his seat. "We land in fifteen minutes."

Pup tilted his head in acknowledgment, and the attendant nodded before turning to Elena. He cast a glance back at Pup, who shook his head subtly.

"I got it." Knowing Elena didn't need a stranger waking her from her pretend nap, he'd bite the bullet.

No, he wanted to be the one to do that. So, he reached out, pulling the lever to tilt the seat upright, then stood with a slow, deliberate stretch that sent a pleasant pull from his middle. He strolled over to Elena and knelt by the couch where she was lying, just like the flight attendant had done to him.

"Elena, honey—" Did he really just call her honey?

Her body stiffened with a sudden tension, warning him she'd heard him loud and clear.

He cleared his throat, trying to steady himself.

"Elena, we're landing soon. You need to wake."

When her eyes fluttered open, he almost blurted out "faker"—but caught himself. Showing that kind of immaturity was beneath him. Instead, he offered a small smile and stood. "You were tired, weren't you?"

She yawned broadly, then sat up. She nodded silently, refusing to meet his gaze, and ran her fingers through her long, dark hair.

Pup took a cautious step back, eyes sharp, watching her subtle movements. She was clearly avoiding him, and he desperately wanted to know why. But he knew better than to press. His sisters had taught him that much about women, and knowing when to ask and when to remain silent.

Before settling into his seat, Pup carefully buckled Casey's harness into the seat belt clip, ensuring she was secure for the descent. With a confident nod, he then settled back into his seat, fastening his seat belt as the plane prepared for landing. The atmosphere was tense, and he wasn't sure how to break the ice.

"Did I sleep the entire flight?" Elena's voice was tinged with disbelief as she nestled into the middle of the couch. She carefully buckled Tiki into the space beside her before securing her seatbelt.

Pup gently petted Casey, encouraging her to lie down and relax. It was her first flight, and the sudden pressure changes had unsettled her, leaving the K9 restless.

Tiki whimpered softly, her distress clear. Elena, alert and compassionate, gently reached beneath her blanket to retrieve a well-loved rope toy. Smiling softly, she offered it to Tiki. "Here you go." Then she turned to Pup. "Give her something to chew on."

Nodding, Pup unbuckled his seat belt and stood, moving to his carry-on stowed above. After retrieving a chew toy from the side pocket, he returned to Casey, the K9's eager eyes tracking his movements.

Pup handed the toy to Casey, who attempted to tear it up. Laughing, Pup sat and buckled himself into his seat, giving a thumbs-up to the flight attendant who'd leaned around the wall separating the crew from the passengers.

"Is someone meeting us at the airport?" He suspected they wouldn't have a vehicle of their own since they were traveling again in two days.

"Yes." Elena threw back her shoulders, stretching and pushing her breasts forward.

Pup knew it was unintentional, but he couldn't help but stare where he shouldn't. Damn, she had a captivating chest.

Things remained tense and a bit awkward until after they landed and started unbuckling the dogs.

Elena shot him a look. "Look, I'm sorry for not being kinder earlier."

Pup blinked, caught off guard by the apology, and nodded slowly. He playfully tilted his head. "You mean by locking me out of my building—in the rain, I might add—and then roping my friends into helping you move before telling me you're my new boss?"

Elena rolled her eyes, turning away to grab her carry-on from the overhead bin. "Yeah, that's about right."

Pup chuckled, wondering if there was still hope for their camaraderie—the kind he shared with other HIS agents—fun, caring, yet downright brutal.

Charles and the pilot waved them off warmly as the attendant gently petted Casey, offering a comforting smile before they stepped out of the plane. Pup's smile drooped at the thought of future flights, knowing the dogs might have to be crated—a prospect that didn't sit well with him. But Pup wasn't the one calling the shots. That battle, he knew, was for Elena to fight.

Standing beside a sleek black SUV, a tall man in a sharp black suit waited on the tarmac. When the wind swept through, Pup saw him carrying a gun, his presence intense and commanding. Despite having just arrived on a private flight, their weapons were safely stowed away in their checked luggage—an inconvenience but necessary, according to the TSA. Seeing him armed ignited a restless urge in Pup to wear his weapon, the tension thick in the air.

Elena and Tiki guided them to the man who introduced himself simply as Aaron, motioning for them to step into the vehicle. A crew member swiftly unloaded their bags from the plane, tossing them into the back of the SUV.

Pup stared in disbelief. Elena had packed only one large suitcase. Sure, he'd packed the same, but he always imagined women needed more space—after all, wasn't it all about their beauty routines? Makeup, accessories, the endless quest to look perfect—wasn't that what filled their bags? It had his sisters'.

Aaron smiled confidently as he smoothly exited the tarmac and glided through a sleek gate for private flights. "After we check you into the hotel, you'll have some time to rest before we head to the venue to get a feel for the space. Zee's performing tonight and tomorrow night, so we'll need a quick sweep before each show to ensure everything's clean."

Pup gazed out the window, watching the diverse California landscape unfold, while Aaron expertly navigated the busy, relentless traffic, the anticipation mounting with every mile.

"I'm not sure why they sent both of you, but honestly, we'll take all the help we can get." He offered a reassuring glance at Elena sitting beside him. "It'll ease Zee's mind."

Elena turned to the back seat, her hand gently petting Tiki, who sat upright and buckled next to Pup, crammed between the K9s. She looked back at Aaron. "Have there been any new threats?"

He shook his head, voice steady. "Don't worry. We've got that covered."

"But—" Elena started to protest, but Aaron quickly cut her off.

"We've got it covered. Your only job is ensuring her performance sites and hotel rooms are clear."

Pup's instinct was to shout that they could do more, but he knew better than to push. That was Elena's battle, and clearly, now was not the time to fight it.

"Okay." Elena slowly drew back and gazed out the front window, her body stiff as a board.

Pup could sense the tension. She'd shut herself off from Tiki. He watched her, feeling a mix of concern and curiosity.

Pup tried to lighten the mood. "What are we to do in

our downtime?" Maybe they could do a little sightseeing —though honestly, he wasn't longing to see anything in particular in Sacramento, but the idea of some freedom, some adventure, sparked a flicker of hope in him.

"You're really on a tight leash." Aaron turned into a hotel. "Any moment, you need to be ready to sweep whatever location Zee chooses to visit if she wishes it."

Unfrickenbelievable.

Elena shifted in her seat. Pup observed her furrowed brows. "If it's not on the schedule, why bother sweeping? It's not like anyone would suspect she'd be there and plant a device."

Aaron shook his head, a hint of concern shadowing his eyes. "I get it, but Zee's scared right now. Anything that helps her relax so she can perform—that's what we do."

At that moment, even knowing they'd have lush accommodations, Pup realized this mission was going to be a challenge—and not the good kind.

They pulled up to the valet, where two men dressed just like Aaron—Pup only brought one suit, hoping he wouldn't have to wear it constantly—waited to help. As the valets unloaded the trunks, Aaron ignored the bustling hotel staff, his eyes fixed on Elena, Tiki, Pup, and Casey as they stepped into the most lavish hotel Pup had ever seen, each detail more stunning than the last.

"I've already checked you in." Aaron glanced between his clones and the guests. He produced two sleek plastic cards, flashing a reassuring smile. "Here are your room keys." He handed one to each of them, his movements smooth and practiced.

But Elena's voice sliced through the moment, sharp and curious. "Wait a second." She narrowed her eyes. "Did you just say 'room?' As in one?"

Exasperated, Aaron exhaled sharply, his eyes narrowing as he read the information. "Yes, it's a two-bedroom suite, one of the hotel's finest, or so I've been told. Is that a problem?"

Pup knew it was because Elena tightened her grip on Tiki's leash. He wanted to diffuse the situation before Elena let out a string of her Spanish curses. "Nope. We're fine with it."

Elena turned to him, her eyes narrowing to a sharp, commanding glare, as if chastising him for speaking out of turn. But she'd soon realize that while she might be his superior, they were ultimately a team.

Aaron glanced at his watch, then nodded toward one of his men. "All right. You two need to be at the hotel lobby by four sharp. Have your K9s prepared." He fixed them with a piercing look. "And, I hope you've got better attire to wear."

Elena and Pup each cast a glance down at their clothing, Pup's mind racing. It had been a long flight, and they had each slipped into their familiar HIS T-shirts and sturdy black cargo pants. Pup's eyes lingered on their attire, and he saw no reason to worry as they weren't part of Aaron's official team, just outside hires, contractors.

"We'll be fine." Pup didn't fully feel that confidence, cutting Elena off before she could voice her concern. He caught a flicker of fear in her eyes, creating a knot in his stomach. Had she forgotten to pack a business suit? That was standard for formal missions since most clients wanted weapons out of sight. But they usually wore the black HIS T-shirts under their jackets, a simple, unwavering uniform.

As they neared the elevator, Pup could almost see Elena's frantic thoughts racing. "You didn't pack a suit, did you?"

She sighed, eyes closing briefly. "No."

Pup chuckled softly. "That's okay. If there's one thing my sisters have drilled into me, it's how to hunt down the best clothes without breaking the bank."

Exiting the elevator on the ninth floor, they strode down a lengthy corridor, where doors were spaced farther apart than usual—an entire floor dedicated to suites. Stopping in front of door 912, Elena pulled out her card key, her voice tinged with frustration. "One damn room."

Pup nearly chuckled. "Well, at least the dogs get to play together."

Elena turned, raising an eyebrow. "As long as we're not 'playing.'"

Pup caught her subtle hint and smiled mischievously. "Now, imagine how dull the trip would be without a little fun?"

Her eyes widened, and Pup burst into laughter. Suddenly, the trip didn't seem so bad after all.

Chapter Fourteen

Elena tossed her purse on the bed and dropped the suitcase handle before collapsing onto the soft mattress, stomach first. She longed to bury her face in the pillows and scream her frustration at the four walls. Why only one shared hotel suite? She forced herself to think positively —at least they had separate rooms. Not that she was worried about him bothering her, not in that way.

It was just...well, she cherished her privacy. It had been so long since she truly had it that she yearned to hold on to it again. But she reminded herself that this was only temporary. They'd be flying to Las Vegas for a concert in a couple of days, then back to Baltimore.

A groan escaped her as she recalled Aaron's comment about their outfits and Pup's readiness to help. Unlike many women, she despised shopping, especially for clothes. Now, she wished she'd had a jacket. What had she been thinking? Probably nothing, she realized, except that Pup had muddled her mind.

That thought wrung another groan from her again. Why was she so worried about that man? He was the last untimely and enigmatic trouble she needed right now.

A sharp knock echoed at her door, causing Elena's head to snap toward it.

"Everything okay in there?"

She narrowed her eyes, already annoyed by the invasion of her privacy. She couldn't even let out a self-indulgent groan without someone barging in. "I'm fine." Though she wasn't. But he—of all people—didn't need to know the truth.

"Good. Listen, we need to move fast if we're going to get you something to wear before our sweep time."

Well, hell. It was a lost cause, and she knew it was her damn fault. She should've expected they'd want their weapons concealed, though she was accustomed to leaving them out in the open as a warning.

Tiki whined. She hated that they'd leave the dogs in the suite together, but they couldn't bring them in these bustling crowds of shoppers. "It's okay, girl. We won't be long."

Climbing from the bed, she grabbed her purse and smoothed the strands of escaping hair from her ponytail. She'd have to suffice as she was because she wasn't getting dolled up to shop.

With her K9 trailing closely behind, they exited the room to Pup, who leaned over, whispering to Casey. It was clear he hated leaving the dog behind, and oddly enough, that made her like him just a little more.

She paused suddenly. No, that wasn't right—she wasn't about to get attached again. She'd just ended a relationship. She wasn't jumping into another one anytime soon.

Wait—where were her thoughts drifting? He was

too young, her subordinate, and probably a notorious playboy since he was still single.

Her mind flashed to the woman at his apartment almost as if on cue. Okay, maybe he wasn't exactly single anymore.

She shook off the lingering memory and shifted her focus to the task at hand—her outfit. "I'm ready." She adjusted her small, black crossbody purse. Despite her calm exterior, seeing him still made her smile wryly. Neither of them had changed, yet they looked like a couple of mercenaries ready for a secret mission.

She winced at the thought, her voice gentle but firm. "We'd best leave our weapons locked in the hotel room's safe. Open carrying in Sacramento isn't wise—especially since it's illegal."

Nodding quickly, Pup stood up and went back to his room, walking with purpose. He returned and extended his weapon, his eyes locked onto hers. "The safe must be in your room because it's not in mine or out here."

It was clear he was always one step ahead—dammit.

She nodded, though she wasn't sure if the safe was in her room. Without hesitation, she turned and charged into her space, eyes scanning. Sure enough, tucked inside the tiny closet, the safe awaited. She set a code with swift fingers, locking away their guns, though she hated to be unarmed, even if the outing was shopping and not a threat.

After instructing Casey and Tiki to wait, they went downstairs and approached the concierge's desk.

Pup turned to ask a few quick questions before leaving a tip.

Stepping out into the blazing sun and brisk cold, they felt a cool gust of wind, almost as cold as Baltimore.

Pup pointed eagerly to the left. "Let's head this way. Paul says there's a fantastic collection of women's boutiques down that street."

Elena's mind immediately jumped to the idea of expensive shops, and she couldn't shake the worry about fancy shops more than Pup had a girlfriend.

She inwardly groaned, scolding herself for her mind drifting back to the topic. To clear her thoughts, she decided to ask him something—anything. Anything but "Do you have a girlfriend?" So, she went with, "Paul?"

Nodding, Pup carefully shifted to her other side, positioning himself to safeguard between her and the bustling road. She couldn't help but think how adorable his protectiveness was.

"Yeah, the concierge." He gave a small smile.

It all made sense now. Why hadn't she remembered the man's name? Because I was foolishly scanning the hotel like some threat could leap out at any moment—stupidly on edge and missing the obvious.

Elena sighed, her shoulders sagging in frustration. "Just a quick thank you before I forget—thanks for doing this."

Pup chuckled softly, his eyes twinkling with mischief.

"What?" Elena's brow furrowed. "What's so funny?"

Pup grinned. "That sounded like that movie with the prostitute and the rich guy."

Elena stopped mid-step, confusion flickering across

her face. Her voice sharpened with surprise and a hint of offense. "Are you calling me a prostitute?"

Pup held up his hands defensively. "No, no! I was just saying—she did that before he took her out or something."

The memory of that film suddenly surfaced in Elena's mind. Everyone knew that story. But beneath her calm exterior, a twinge of suspicion crept in. Was he comparing her? Her nerves, already frayed by everything else, now felt like they were about to snap.

"Did you know that a dog's nose print is as unique as a human fingerprint?"

Before she could respond, Pup suddenly stopped, a grin on his face. "Here's the first suggestion, though he actually had three, so there's no need to settle for the first store."

She rolled her eyes, silently counting her needs, especially a jacket. She didn't care whether she genuinely liked it. This was for work. She wondered if the Hamilton brothers would even approve her expense, nearly laughing at the thought.

"Okay." She kept her voice light as he held the door open for her. A gentleman to the core. "Where were you raised?" She hesitated after asking the personal question. What was she doing?

"Pensacola, Florida." He followed her into the cozy, inviting shop. "My dad was a Navy pilot, stationed there most of his career."

She thought of the itinerary she'd been given, her brows knitting in thought. "Isn't Pensacola one of our stops?" Her tone was tinged with surprise, hinting that her curiosity had deepened. She paused at the first rack, her eyes flickering with curiosity. The saleslady's gaze lingered on her with open disdain, reminiscent of the way she had looked at the prostitute in that gritty movie—disapproving. Was it because she was Hispanic or because of how they were dressed? Did the woman think she couldn't afford the place?

"Yep. What size are you?" He examined her from head to toe, making her feel a bit vulnerable. "Six?" Pup's tone was nonjudgmental but knowing.

How? How had he guessed so easily? It was as if the man possessed some hidden skill, more experience than she'd thought. Sisters or not, a man didn't just instinctively know a woman's size—unless he had some secret expertise.

She nodded, a flicker of confidence flashing in her eyes. She wished she could say smaller, but she genuinely appreciated her body just as it was, neither large nor small, perfectly matching her short height. "Yes." She flashed a genuine smile.

"Okay, then." He was already diving into a rack of jackets. "Let's shop."

Before Elena could even scan the racks for something that caught her eye, the saleslady suddenly approached Pup. Elena's irritation flared up. She expected the lady to come to her first, not Pup. It was a women's boutique, after all. However, she decided to let it go. She didn't need the woman's help anyway.

She nearly burst into laughter as Pup waved her off with a dismissive flick of his hand. That was what she deserved for heading to the wrong shopper first—karma catching up most unexpectedly.

Within moments, Pup approached her, clutching a handful of clothing. "I brought some blouses along with the jackets." He shrugged. "Just in case you wanted something a bit more than the HIS T-shirt."

She beamed with pride when she wore the HIS T-shirt, yet she appreciated his thoughtfulness in offering her options. Elena knew Aaron would likely prefer her more "dressed up" than casual, adding more anticipation to her choices.

Ready to sift through the clothes, pick her favorites, and then make a quick exit, Elena jumped when Pup stilled her hand.

"Oh no, try them on first. You need to see if there's enough room under the jackets for your weapon."

He had officially pushed her to the limit. She didn't bother with the usual store antics—trying on clothes in the fitting room was simply not her style. She'd pick out her pieces, buy them, and be done. She'd return or donate them without fuss if they didn't fit. Undressing in some stranger's store behind a locked door? Not her scene.

"That's okay. I can tell." She gave a tight smile back.

Pup tugged the stack of clothing back, a mischievous glint in his eyes. "Come on, live a little, Elena. Try them on." His playful grin stopped her.

She narrowed her eyes, catching on to his game. "You just want a show, don't you?"

He shrugged, flashing a boyish smile. "You got me."

If he wanted a show, she'd give him one. Snatching the clothes from his grasp, Elena spun around and addressed the nosy saleslady. "Your dressing room?"

The woman's eyes lit up at the sight of the pile in Elena's arms, eager to help. Damn. Maybe she should've handled this entire shopping trip herself. Elena silently hoped nothing would fit. Maybe then she wouldn't have to deal with this saleswoman's commission hustle.

In the upscale dressing room where Elena didn't have to worry about bumping her elbows into the wall while trying on clothes, she wondered why she had let him goad her into this. She had a strong will, but this young man was pushing her out of her comfort zone, and she was letting it happen.

What the hell was wrong with her for allowing it?

Ripping off her beloved T-shirt with a sense of anticipation, Elena grabbed the first blouse she liked the most from the stack. She hoped the clothing would fit perfectly, so she wouldn't have to try on every single piece. But as she riffled through the pile, a smile tugged at her lips for the selection Pup had chosen.

She stared at the price tag on the jacket she had paired with the blouse, nearly gagging at the steep cost. Well, she thought, that means buying just two outfits—more than she'd earned in a long while—but it was a sacrifice she'd have to make for this trip. Feeling confident with her choice, she pushed open the dressing room door and stepped out, her eyes searching for Pup, who was lazily sprawled in an armchair nearby, with the saleslady hovering over him.

The woman whispered and giggled softly, her eyes alight with mischief. Pup seemed completely absorbed in their conversation, a slow smile spreading across his face, one she loved. As she studied his expression, a flicker of doubt crossed her mind. Was that smile genuine or just a clever disguise? But then she shrugged, deciding some mysteries were better left unsolved.

Noticing her, he stood, and his gaze moved over her like a scanner. With a mischievous flick of his finger, he invited her to spin, and she raised a brow, unamused.

She wasn't a puppet, after all.

His shoulders slumped in mock submission. "Come on, Elena. Let me see. Turn."

She obliged, a playful smile tugged at her lips as she twirled around. It was fun—so much like that damn movie. That flicker of fear hit her hard, stopping her cold. No way would that be their life. There would be no happy ending for her and Pup.

"Very nice. Very nice indeed." Then, he sat, accepting a beverage from the saleslady with a relaxed smile. "Thank you, Sylvia."

He turned back to Elena. "Next."

Elena, hands on her hips, couldn't believe the nerve. Thank you, Sylvia. She couldn't believe this. He was flirting with the saleslady, who ignored her completely.

"No. I can figure it out from here." Without waiting, she spun around and stormed back to the dressing room, changing back into her HIS T-shirt with a mix of frustration and determination.

Her emotions fluttered wildly today as she navigated her feelings about him. They had subtly shifted—once enemies, then colleagues, and now...perhaps just fellow travelers on this unpredictable journey. She shook her head with a small smile, trying to understand everything.

While sifting through the clothing, her eye caught

two blouses and two jackets, perfect for mixing and matching to refresh her look. She'd also have the blouses she'd brought along, each piece a small anchor amid the chaos of her thoughts.

Leaving the dressing room, she caught sight of the saleslady still fussing over Pup. Nausea rose, sharp and sudden. "Are we ready?" The words came out clipped, her patience scraped thin.

The saleslady glanced at the handful of clothing in her arms, furrowing her brow. "Is that it?"

Elena clenched her fists, fighting the urge to toss the clothes on the floor and storm out. She knew it would only mean starting the whole process over again, so she hesitated.

Pup, as if sensing her frustration, stood tall. "You know what." He glanced between her and the saleslady with a determined look. "I think we've wasted enough of your time, Sylvia. Elena, let's go." He extended his hand confidently.

Without hesitation, she handed the clothes to the saleslady and took his hand, eager to leave the store behind.

"How'd you know?" As they stepped outside, she gently let go of his hand.

He shrugged casually. "I got the vibe from her the moment we entered. I'd hoped she'd change her tune."

Elena couldn't hide her astonishment at how perceptive he'd been. "Thank you. I hate shopping, but I despised that lady's attitude toward me even more."

"That's okay. There are more stores." Pup scanned the bustling street as they turned a corner. "We'll find you something Aaron won't look down upon."

He'd realized that, too. Every moment they spent together was a chance to impress her. Her initial concern about his maturity—considering his age—faded away. He wasn't just a young man. He was all man. And that mixture of fright and excitement within her was new.

What's the next twist in their evolving relationship? Well, not that kind of relationship—just a professional, civil colleague connection, she mused.

"Did you know dogs have about seventeen hundred taste buds, while humans have around nine thousand?"

She couldn't help but smile. And that was her undoing.

Chapter Fifteen

Pup plopped onto the bed, giving his belly a gentle pat, inviting Casey to join him. "Girl, I'm wiped out." He sighed. After a whirlwind day of shopping—finding Elena four stylish blouses, two jackets, and another small piece of luggage—they grabbed a quick bite at a small sidewalk cafe. Now, they were back, ready to rest before their big debut.

All in all, it had been a pretty good day—except for the awkward moment when the first saleslady flirted with him right in front of Elena. That stung more than it should have, but Elena's reaction told a different story. Maybe Elena's upset hadn't been Sylvia hitting on him, but Sylvia ignoring her instead. He'd have to figure out why, especially since a similar situation had cropped up before they even found the right store.

As Casey jumped onto the bed beside him, face pressed against his gut, he smoothed her fur. "Did you miss me, girl?"

The dog whined softly in response, and Pup chuckled at their little exchange.

There was something different about Elena today—

something that told him she wasn't the bitch on wheels woman he'd previously seen. Sure, impatience flooded her, but so did kindness. He recalled how she'd overtipped the server at lunch, upset by another customer's rudeness that nearly brought the server to tears.

She had a heart, no doubt.

Yet, she'd still swooped in and taken the job that should've been his.

He groaned. "When am I going to let that go?" he whispered, careful to keep Elena from hearing his frustration from the other room.

He couldn't change that fact, so stressing over it was pointless. If things didn't work out with Elena as his boss, he'd just find another place to work. It was that simple. But deep down, he loved HIS, the Hamilton family, and all the agents.

As if on cue, his phone rang, pulling him from his thoughts. Retrieving it from his pocket, he saw the caller ID and looked at Casey, smirking. "This ought to be good." He answered. "What's up, Cowboy?"

"Howdy! How's everything hanging on your end of the country?"

Pup chuckled, their quick check-in confirmed he was still all right. It was his first adventure without the others, and it was also Casey's first test. They didn't trust him alone, yet.

"It's all good." Pup gently petted Casey's head. Her big brown eyes met his, unwavering. She was so trusting. He wouldn't let her down.

"I bet. So, how's the new boss?"

Pup wanted to groan. That was it. They—and he

knew there was a "they" behind this call—wanted to know about Elena, not how he was really doing. That kicked him in the gut. The question hung in the air, heavy with unspoken truths and frustrations, making Pup feel the familiar sting of being misunderstood yet again.

"She's fine." After a brief hesitation, he had no idea what he was about to say. "But she's an impatient shopper." His hand froze on Casey's shoulder. Why had he said that? Was he deliberately trying to tarnish Elena's reputation in the eyes of the men? No. He couldn't be that petty.

"Shopper?" Cowboy's grin bled through his voice. "I thought ya guys were on the clock, not on vacation." He chuckled warmly. "Has she been dragging you sightseeing, too?"

Pup didn't bother correcting him about who was dragged shopping. Cowboy's humor was good, and it wasn't worth spoiling the moment. "Nah, man. The security lead here is a prick, and she needed some proper attire."

"Hmm."

"What?" Pup's brows shot up.

"Well, I'm a wondering why you had to go shopping with her. Did she make you?"

"Nah, man. It's just—" A flicker of hesitation paused him as he searched for the right words. "Honestly, I was just bored and didn't want to sit in the hotel room." He needed to change the subject before he said something he shouldn't. "So, how's the wife and kid?"

Cowboy, a confirmed bachelor, had fallen for his handyman and her little boy—a surprising twist he enjoyed sharing. Watching his friend navigate those turbulent waters had been more entertaining than he expected.

A genuine smile crept into Cowboy's voice as he reminisced about the mischievous things the kid had done, his tone warm with affection.

Pup shook his head and rolled his eyes toward Casey, a silent acknowledgment that he'd never imagined their conversations would drift into talk about children. He and Cowboy had spent countless nights at bars, chasing women and living in the moment. That world of endless nights and fleeting romances felt so distant now, replaced, perhaps, by something unexpectedly real.

Pup felt a sharp ache in his chest from the loss of Cowboy as his wingman, lost to vows and vows alone. Most of the guys had moved on—married, in serious relationships, or claiming they were "too old for the bar scene." The last night Pup tried to go out after losing his job was a solo mission, ending with him calling his sister to drag his drunken self home. It boded ill—a lonely chapter in his life. Maybe someone on the new Charlie team….

As if realizing he'd lost Pup, Cowboy cleared his throat, the weight of the moment settling in. "Anyhow, we were just checking in on ya. If ya need anything, just say the word."

Pup ended the call, shutting it off before the conversation drifted back to Elena. A pang of guilt flickered. He couldn't shake the feeling that his little "impatient shopper" remark had stabbed her in the back. Sure, he knew the agents would get a kick out of it, but how would Elena feel when they started calling her something like "Patience?"

He shrugged off the concern. If she couldn't handle a little ribbing, maybe she wasn't cut out for this. Period. But, Patience fit.

Checking his watch, he realized rest was a luxury he couldn't afford before showtime. A long, hot shower suddenly sounded like the perfect escape. "Let me up, girl."

Casey, clueless about the change in mood, cocked her head.

Pup chuckled. This was one clever dog. She was trying to decipher the conversation—at least, that's what Pup decided her maneuver meant.

He pushed the dog's head off his gut. "I'll let you remain on the bed this once. But only this once."

Casey stayed put, not caring if she wasn't allowed on it.

Shaking his head, Pup stood and stretched, his arms high above his head. The stretch in his midsection felt good.

After a quick shower, he slipped into slacks and HIS T-shirt, the one that felt most natural against his skin. He added his shoulder harness. He preferred a drop leg holster, but he figured Aaron wanted their weapons covered, so shoulder harness it was. Then, he reluctantly tugged on the dreaded sports jacket. It gave him some room to maneuver, but in his mind, it still felt restrictive. The T-shirt alone was his favorite—comfortable and effortless. Yet, he knew better than to push his luck today, especially since Aaron oversaw this operation.

He paused, pondering how Elena would handle Aaron's apparent distaste for her. It hadn't helped that he'd already shown his disapproval. Sure, her attire was the issue, but after witnessing the way people had treated her earlier, he couldn't shake the unease settling in him.

Why were people treating her differently? Was it because she looked like a mercenary, or was it because she was Hispanic? He sincerely hoped it wasn't the latter because he despised racism in any form. A flicker of resolve sparked within him. He'd need to watch how Aaron and the team interacted with her to ensure she was treated fairly. Then, a new thought emerged. When had it become his personal mission to make sure she felt welcome on this operation?

Then it hit him like a ton of bricks—he cared how she was treated. And it wasn't just about his preconceived notions or that she was HIS. No, he genuinely cared, and that realization caught him off guard. He'd only just met her, and their interaction had been far from pretty. How could he already feel—

The sharp rap on his suite bedroom door abruptly snapped Pup out of his racing thoughts.

"Ready?"

Nodding to himself, Pup took a deep breath and examined himself in the mirror one last time. He wondered if Aaron would approve of their clothes, but he was more curious about what the man thought of his earring. Aaron hadn't even looked Pup's way when they arrived, so he probably hadn't noticed. Tonight, Pup decided, he'd find out what Aaron was really made of.

"I'm coming." He patted his leg to beckon Casey

over. Over time, he'd been training her with nonverbal cues, and now he saw the fruits of his patience. She responded, gently hopping off the bed, her tail wagging eagerly as she approached him, a sparkle in her eyes.

"Whoa there, girl. It's not playtime now. This is the real deal."

Casey barked excitedly, and Pup burst into laughter. He knew he should keep the dog quiet in the hotel, but her pure joy in working was contagious. He hoped—and expected—they'd find nothing, but it would still be fantastic training for Casey. Plus, he'd get to see Tiki shine outside of training sessions. Silently, he'd been in awe of the K9—jealous, yet incredibly inspired.

Opening the door to his room, he paused, eyes narrowing as he caught Elena in the act. She was attaching Tiki's leash to her dog's vest and slapping on the "Explosives Detection" patch on each side of the harness.

Pup attached Casey's leash to her harness, attached her patches, and stood there. He nearly did a double-take, knocked on his ass.

Elena looked…stunning. She'd put on makeup and left her hair down instead of in the ponytail or braid she normally sported.

His breath caught in his chest. "You look beautiful."

Beneath her olive-toned skin, he noticed a faint blush creeping up her cheeks.

He chuckled softly, appreciating this side of her— the gentle woman he hadn't yet really known but wanted to. "You blushed."

She narrowed her eyes, denying it fiercely. "I did

not."

Pup's grin grew wider. That was the Elena he knew and expected for this mission—full of fire and ice. He wasn't sure he'd want it any other way. Once again, that caught him off guard. What the hell?

"Now." Her smile snuck into his heart. "Let's get this show on the road."

Pup nodded, sensing it was best to follow her lead. With a silent agreement, he trailed her out of the room, down the corridor, and into the elevator. As the doors slid shut, Pup took a deep breath and was hit by a delightful, heavenly scent wafting in from her. She'd added perfume to her ensemble. Well, well. He hadn't pegged her as a scrub muffin, but with makeup, a fresh hairstyle, and that alluring fragrance—who was this transformed woman he worked with?

"Whatever you're doing back there, cut it out."

Behind her, Pup's grin widened, hinting at mischief. Oh yeah, this was about to get interesting. "I'm just standing here." He wasn't sure his innocent act would succeed.

She inhaled sharply, glancing over her shoulder with suspicion. "Uh-huh."

Pup chuckled, a little too confident. "Truly."

She waved a dismissive hand. "Whatever."

The elevator doors opened with a soft ding, and Aaron stood there, glancing at his watch with a hint of impatience. "You're late." He crossed his arms across his chest.

Elena glanced at her watch. "Actually, mine says we're right on time." Her eyes glinted with a challenge.

Pup's back stiffened, muscles taut, ready to jump in and diffuse the tension, but Aaron's gaze swept over her, calm and measured.

After a moment, he simply nodded. "Let's go." He turned sharply as if the exchange hadn't happened, leaving the air thick with unspoken words.

Catching up alongside Elena and Tiki, Pup leaned in. "Do you think it's wise to provoke our boss on this mission?"

Elena spun around, eyes blazing with conviction. "Don't tell me how to do my job. He's an ass, and I won't stand for bullying."

Pup hadn't considered Aaron's behavior as bullying, but from Elena's perspective, it clearly was. He hesitated, then nodded. "All right." He stepped back a bit with Casey.

He was drawn to Elena's fiery spirit, the kind that lit a room and dared you closer. Yet, beneath that fiery exterior, a worry gnawed at him. He couldn't shake the sense that if she responded to any interaction with that same fire, the rest of the mission might be severely affected.

Chapter Sixteen

They approached the massive stage where Zee was set to perform. Elena turned to Pup. "Let's see Casey in action. Circle the perimeter first."

"We already know what to do," he snapped.

Elena narrowed her eyes, irritation flickering. What was his problem? She had only told him to get started. Shrugging it off, she focused. She couldn't afford to argue with Pup right now, especially with Aaron's eyes fixed on them. Since they'd arrived at the hotel lobby, he'd barely taken his gaze off her.

On the ride to the venue, he'd kept sneaking looks at her in the passenger seat, which was downright unnerving.

She understood he wasn't thrilled about her and Pup tagging along, but still….

Tiki whined softly beside her, clearly displeased at being relegated to the background on the job. Once she carefully placed the harness and patches on Tiki, the K9 was more than ready to get to work—she wasn't interested in trailing behind a pup in training.

Elena almost chuckled at the irony of it all. Who was

really in training here? Pup or Casey? Maybe both. And it was up to her to figure out what each of them needed to succeed, whether Pup wanted to accept it or not.

After circling the perimeter, Pup confidently led Casey up the stage steps, his focus sharp and unwavering.

Elena trailed behind with Tiki, silent but attentive, letting Pup maintain his concentration on his young K9 partner. The seamless teamwork between Pup and the trainee spoke volumes about Pup's impressive skills and dedication in guiding a young K9 in training.

Surveying the area, Elena's gaze settled on a janitor watching them intently. It was common for onlookers to observe K9s in action, but this man's stare gave her an uneasy feeling, crawling under her skin. Maybe it was harmless, or maybe it signaled something more. She decided she'd have Aaron check him out. If he would listen to her suspicions. Was the guy just a creeper? That didn't mean he was a threat or was bad at his job. He might just be doing his duty.

Still, Elena couldn't shake the feeling that something was off, especially since Aaron had made it clear—they were only to scan the area, not investigate the threatening messages. A simple observation or something more? Elena's heart pounded with curiosity and caution.

Suddenly, Casey froze, sat down abruptly, and let out a whine. Tiki pulled free from Elena and sniffed eagerly around Casey, mirroring the same alarmed behavior. An unsettling silence settled before Elena whispered, "Holy shit." It was then that she realized— they had just uncovered an explosive.

Instinct kicked in. "Everyone out!" Her voice was

firm and commanding, splitting the air. "Now!"

Aaron rushed to her side, concern and confusion written all over his face. "Are you out of your mind?"

"Pup, slowly back away with Casey. Tiki will follow." She scanned the chaos. She hated that the dog had broken free from her grip, but was relieved that she was trained in team commands, giving her a slight edge in the tense moment.

"What's going on?"

Elena spun around to Aaron, eyes blazing with fury. "The dogs found a bomb."

Aaron's face drained of color. "Impossible. No one had access to this venue without my trusted security team."

Elena's posture stiffened, her voice sharp. "Then what the hell did you hire us for if not to check behind your 'trusted' team?"

Aaron studied her, irritation flickering in his eyes. He turned sharply to the throng still milling around.

Elena's thoughts buzzed with frustration. Stupid assholes, she grumbled. She had a K9 with an "Explosive Detection" patch and had loudly instructed everyone to evacuate, yet a stubborn few lingered.

Aaron's voice held a commanding authority. "Everyone out! There's a bomb!"

Elena shut her eyes briefly, suppressing the urge to say the word aloud. Mentioning "bomb" tended to stir panic, and that was a chaos she desperately wanted to avoid.

Pup stood silently by her side, his eyes scanning the area with sharp focus. She sensed he missed nothing, every detail registering in his vigilant gaze. Her mind raced. Did he notice the janitor, who was now missing from his usual spot by the mop bucket? At least he had listened to her. Or….

"There was a janitor—"

Aaron quickly interrupted her, his tone firm and urgent. "Just look for bombs. We've already vetted this staff."

"Just like your team secured that area?" She hadn't meant to snap at him. The man's composure was fraying, and when he pulled out his phone, her eyes flicked to it with suspicion. "What are you planning to do with that?"

"Call the police, of course." She caught the hint of defiance in his voice.

She hesitated, almost reaching for the phone, but a realization snapped into her mind—she wasn't a police officer anymore, and her job depended on playing it smart. She softened her tone just a bit. "Let's take this outside before you make that call."

Aaron took a deep breath, silence hanging in the air, before he nodded firmly. Without hesitation, he turned on his heels and led the way, decisive and sure.

Elena glanced at Pup, whose eyes shifted from the two looming security guards to her, questioning. She raised an eyebrow, seeking reassurance. Pup shook his head slightly. "We're ready." His voice was low and steady.

After the foursome hurried out of the building, they rewarded the dogs with their favorite toys. But all eyes were on Aaron as he remained engrossed in his phone. The staff around them murmured, their whispers tinged with curiosity. Yet, the tension had escalated when Aaron uttered the word "bomb." Instantly, a ripple of panic had spread. What he said was now destined for the news.

Elena had Tiki settle down before she fished her phone out of her pocket. It was time to make a call. She tapped a preset button, her finger poised as she waited for the video call to connect. The screen flickered, and Devon's face lit up her phone.

"Hey, Elena! How's the vacation?" A warm smile spread across his face.

She rolled her eyes, and Devon chuckled. "We're working." Elena sensed the playfulness in her voice. Then, she became serious. "And, we've discovered something…."

Devon sat up straighter. "Something like what, exactly?"

She paused for effect. "A bomb."

"Let me get Jesse." Devon turned away from the screen.

A moment later, Jesse appeared, his expression tense. "What's this about a bomb?"

"Casey and Tiki both lit up on the stage floor." She kept her voice steady but urgent. "Since it was just a crawl space, we didn't go underneath, but something had to be hidden there."

Jesse furrowed his brow, concern shadowing his features. "How did Aaron take it?"

Elena scoffed, a sharp edge in her tone. "You mean the man who shouted 'bomb' to the crowd?" She crossed her free arm across her chest.

Jesse shook his head slowly, eyes still focused. "I

worried about that man."

Elena's eyes narrowed. "And yet, you sent us here?" Realizing her tone might have been too harsh, she softened slightly. "He's not exactly a saint to work with."

"Zee is our client, and we like her. Aaron's just the go-between, but I'm sorry if he's made your life miserable."

"That's an understatement."

"Well, let's see how this plays out. They'll probably cancel the concert, of course. But maybe—they'll be more forgiving to you and Pup now that you've saved her life."

Elena realized she hadn't considered the bigger picture—she'd just saved Zee's life, along with her backup singers, band, and stage crew. She'd been blinded by the red haze of anger at Aaron, missing the implications of their actions.

"How are Pup and Casey doing?" Jesse leaned in with genuine concern.

Elena flashed a quick smile as her eyes caught Pup, who was scanning the crowd with focused intensity, clearly ignoring their conversation. "She was the first to light on it. I was quite impressed." Elena's voice was tinged with pride.

A moment of hesitation crossed her mind. She shouldn't boast too much about Pup's skills, or they might start questioning if they'd hired the right lead handler. But then, she shook off the petty doubt, realizing Pup's talent deserved recognition. She tucked her pride away and allowed herself a small smile of genuine admiration for her partner.

"Good. We thought they were ready to be on their own. Maybe now we don't need the two of you there. You can come back, leaving them to handle the operation."

Elena's brow furrowed as she listened. On one hand, she was relieved about not working with Aaron anymore. On the other hand, she hesitated. After the shopping excursion, she wanted to stay close to Pup. She couldn't quite explain it, but his company felt…right. When he wasn't being a smartass.

"That's your call. But if we're not needed, I can still work with them to uncover just how capable they really are."

Jesse glanced off-screen. "Do we need the K9 units for the upcoming operation?"

Elena's stomach flipped as Devon answered. "No."

Turning back to her, Jesse's smile was reassuring. "Okay, Elena. We'll leave both of you there, but if Aaron becomes too much to handle, call me. I won't tolerate my agents being anything less than respected."

That simple gesture warmed Elena's heart. She was grateful to have found such a supportive company. "Thanks, Jesse."

They ended the call, and Elena turned to Pup with a curious look. "How's it coming?" She knew he was busy searching, not ignoring her call, but seeking something or someone out of the ordinary.

He shook his head slowly and glanced at her. "Nothing so far."

Elena's mind immediately jumped to the suspicious janitor. She scanned the crowd, but he was nowhere to be seen. She'd have to discuss that with Aaron—if he'd listen.

"What's the verdict?" Pup petted Casey, who held her toy in her mouth.

"We're staying for now." She swallowed the truth that she'd had every opportunity to leave but chose not to. Instead, she'd crafted an intricate plan to stay close to Pup and Casey, almost like a secret mission. Why?

Pup raised an eyebrow playfully. "What do you think of Casey now?"

She smiled warmly. "She's on her way to becoming a hero." She possessed a teasing sparkle in her eye. "Just like Tiki, here."

Pup rolled his eyes but couldn't suppress a chuckle. "So, it's like that, huh?"

In that moment, Elena realized she'd made the right choice. Staying by their side felt right. The camaraderie among teammates was something she'd never truly known before with SWAT. Now, she was finally beginning to find it, and she was eager to hold onto this feeling for as long as she could.

She wondered if there was an ulterior motive behind her decision to stay by their side—something beyond genuine camaraderie.

The realization hit her hard.

She was so screwed.

Chapter Seventeen

Pup was over the moon. Pride swelled inside him as Casey made her latest find. Finding an explosive was serious business, but her success was a cause for celebration. Just a year old, she was already proving to be a star with two impressive finds under her collar. Pup couldn't contain his excitement to see her in action. He knew she'd excel in search and rescue, too.

They made their way back to the hotel, the tension still lingering in the vehicle. Chaos had erupted when word spread that a bomb had been found, sending people scrambling to evacuate the arena. It's a strange irony—sometimes, it takes a crisis for folks to finally act.

Aaron repeated himself for what felt like the hundredth time. "I still can't believe you actually found a bomb." The man struggled to focus on the road, leaving nerves prickling at Pup's skin, but Pup knew he was at Aaron's mercy. He was the boss on this operation.

Elena sat quietly in the passenger seat, her calm presence giving Pup a small surge of confidence, reassuring him that Aaron's jitters wouldn't distract him from the road.

Pup sat between Casey and Tiki, gently stroking each of them, wary of any alpha tendencies that might prompt one to leap from the pack. These two dogs were more than just companions—they might just be forming their own pack. If only they had Charlie's team K9, they could become a formidable force. Well, they did have the K9, but he was reserved for "special operations." That thought set his teeth to grind. Casey was just as ready as Buddy and should have been involved in these critical missions that Charlie team seemed to undertake. Yet, jealousy simmered inside him, a bitter taste he couldn't swallow.

"Well." Elena's voice was steady, and Pup appreciated it. "We did. Now, can we talk about those letters?"

Aaron shook his head. "My security team and the police are handling them."

Elena peered over her shoulder, subtly checking on Tiki and catching Pup's brief eye-roll with a smile. Then she turned back to Aaron, her gaze unwavering. "What's the plan now?"

Meanwhile, Pup lingered on Elena's smile, lost in thought. As the two continued talking about Zee canceling her tour—which meant they might head home —Pup's mind drifted. Did he want to go? No, he realized deeply—he only truly wanted Elena. He remembered the moment he first saw her on his doorstep, fire blazing in her eyes and ice in her veins as she refused him entry, sealing his desire to know her better.

They'd gone from enemies to colleagues—and now the unspoken question hung between them. Could they become friends, maybe even lovers? Not necessarily in that order, of course. He'd be quick to jump into the lover's role before she did something to piss him off again. It would be a love-hate relationship until he accepted that she'd taken his job, and she'd overcome... well, whatever was driving her to be such a bitch at times.

He closed his eyes, swallowing hard. He shouldn't be thinking of her that way. Yet, what other choice did he have?

"So, you two can pack your bags and head out as soon as we get your flight details."

Pup's ears perked up, confusion flickering across his face. Flights? What happened to the private jet?

Elena tilted her head, studying Aaron closely. "Flights? What do you mean?"

"Yeah, two tickets will be sent to your room. We'll get you out as early as we can tomorrow." Aaron pulled into the hotel and brought the SUV to a stop. "Thanks for helping us."

Pup's gut roiled with unease. What the actual fuck was going on? The dogs wouldn't be crammed into kennels in the hold like baggage. They'd walk before that occurred.

Suddenly, Elena's voice cut through the tension. "I'm sorry, Aaron, but that won't work."

Dumbstruck, Aaron looked back at Pup, who shrugged nonchalantly, then his gaze shifted to Elena. "But Zee will need her jet."

"I understand that." Elena gave Aaron a knowing smile. "But our dogs fly in the seats right beside us like service dogs do, so you'll need four seats."

Aaron raised an eyebrow, frustration flickering in his eyes. "That's the dumbest thing I've ever heard."

Elena leaned in slightly, her tone sharp but playful. "Check your contract. It clearly states you'll follow these rules if we're flying commercially. Plus, we handle the flights. So we pick the airlines and seats."

"I suppose it's also first-class."

Elena chuckled softly, her eyes gleaming. "That was your attorney's clever idea."

Pup coughed discreetly to cover up his chuckle, but the grin was hard to suppress.

Elena shot him a sharp, cutting glance before turning back to Aaron with a confident smile. "We'll be out as early as we can." She briskly opened the SUV door. Just before she slipped outside, she looked back at Aaron. "It was nice working with you."

Pup waited patiently as Elena opened the back door for Tiki to exit. Once the dog was out, Pup nodded to Aaron and stepped out, Casey trailing behind him. He stretched lazily as he watched Aaron's vehicle drive away, a small smirk on his face. "Well, that was fun."

"Asshole." Elena's eyes narrowed as she watched the vehicle speed away.

"Hey." Pup turned toward her.

"Not you." Elena pointed at the retreating SUV. "Him."

"I agree. Now, can we eat already? I'm starving."

Elena rolled her eyes but couldn't hide her smirk. "When aren't you?"

He chuckled. "How about room service?" If it was their last night, he was going to see where things went with them. He knew she wanted him. At least, he thought he'd occasionally gotten that vibe from her. She was hard to read, so he hoped he wasn't about to make a fool of himself.

Before entering the hotel, they made a quick stop at a grassy area so the dogs could stretch their legs and take care of their needs. Pup watched Tiki, glancing at her legs, and wondering how she lost one. He decided he'd ask Elena later—right now, a more urgent question was on his mind. "Did you really think we'd find something?"

Elena paused, pondering his question. "No, I figured celebrities get threats all the time. I thought they'd overreacted. Turns out, I'm glad they did."

Pup nodded. "Imagine this—our dogs actually saved the Zee Alvarez. Maybe they're destined for stardom."

Elena chuckled, her eyes sparkling. "Our dogs don't need to be stars. They're heroes. That's all that matters."

In their hotel room, Elena called HIS headquarters, asking someone to check for flights—probably Emily, since she had recently taken on the role of unofficial travel agent, despite her background in forensic accounting.

"Thanks. Can you send—" Elena started, but Pup knew exactly what happened. Emily had already cut her off with an assured "Already done."

"Okay, thanks." Elena ended the call. "Our flight leaves at 0910 tomorrow."

Pup glanced at the room service menu, smirking. "Think Aaron is going to toss in a bonus?" Hungry, he eyed the largest steak on the menu.

Elena chuckled, shaking her head. "After buying four first-class tickets, two for us and two for the dogs? I doubt it. But a guy can dream."

This playful side of Elena shot an arrow straight to his heart. No, it wasn't love—more like a chaotic mix of feelings he shouldn't be having for his boss. Dammit, he'd temporarily forgotten she was his boss. What was the company's policy on fraternization? Did they even have one? He'd never bothered to read that damn manual they'd handed him on his first day.

Hell, he didn't care. Neither should she. He'd convinced himself it was a one-time thing—just a fleeting moment.

Realizing she was gazing at him with expectation in her eyes, he hesitated. "What?"

She shook her head, a gentle sigh escaping her lips. "Have you decided yet?"

He paused, then chuckled, realizing she was talking about the food. "Sure. I'll have the porterhouse." Why not indulge a little when you're about to enjoy the night—or so he hoped.

"Good, I'll have the Cobb Salad. Could you call down and place the order? I want to get out of this getup."

Pup handed her his weapon for the safe. He watched her with a mix of affection and longing. She looked stunning in her new gear, yet he couldn't help but love her in her familiar, HIS gear as well. When he called room service, he also ordered a bottle of wine, unsure of Elena's preferences, to complement their meal—and perhaps what comes after.

Ditching his jacket and harness, he eagerly searched his phone for some mood music. What kind of tunes did Elena prefer? Hip-hop? Probably not. Country?

Hopefully not. He decided a smooth jazz station would be perfect to set the tone. Setting his phone down, he called Casey over to the couch, where he sat. She bounded over happily from her spot with Tiki. He couldn't help but notice how close they seemed to be getting. What would happen when everything returned to normal after the trip?

It was wishful thinking to believe things would go smoothly from here, especially if she wasn't receptive to his advances tonight. Then, it wouldn't be all that comfortable at work anymore. He almost snorted, as if to dismiss the idea, like it hadn't already been that way.

Elena didn't reappear until a knock at the door signaled room service. When the employee wheeled in a cart stacked high with food, Pup's eyes darted to Elena. She stood in her jeans and T-shirt, hair pulled back in a ponytail, yet she still radiated a stunning charm.

"What's all this?"

Pup tipped the server as he left. He grinned. "Thought we could indulge a little."

"Dessert? Wine? Looks like we're going all out—calorie overload."

Pup groaned. "Please tell me you're not one of those who count every calorie?"

Her cheeks flushed as she crossed her arms. "And what if I am?"

Worry infused Pup for the first time in his adult life, and he wondered if he'd completely misread the situation. He quickly tried to brush it off with a mischievous grin. "Honestly, I was hoping to win you over with some charm, then get you drunk so I could have my way with you."

She raised an eyebrow, clearly unimpressed. "I sure hope not."

That ended Pup's fleeting dream of peace between them. He leaned in, voice playful but daring. "Oh, come on. Why not? Am I too young for you?"

She pursed her lips thoughtfully. "Actually, yes. You are a bit young for me."

Pup didn't back down. Before she could react, he was suddenly right in front of her, his hand sliding behind her neck as he pulled her into a close, intense kiss.

For a moment, she didn't pull away, and Pup thought he was winning. That hope shattered when she suddenly pulled back and slapped him hard across the face.

Chapter Eighteen

Elena's eyes widened in shock as her hand flew up. She'd slapped Pup. The moment hung heavy between them. He had kissed her, and suddenly everything felt tangled and forbidden. Was it wrong? Her initial hesitation faded as she found herself responding to the intensity of his kiss, caught in a whirlwind of confusion and unspoken desire.

They couldn't. He was too young in age, not in maturity, and she was his boss. HIS would definitely frown upon it.

Elena's mind spun with a whirlwind of emotions. She couldn't pin down exactly how she felt. Was it anger? Or was it desire? The two battled fiercely in her thoughts, leaving her torn and frantic.

Pup placed his hand on his reddening cheek, a mixture of surprise and delight dancing across his face. "Wow."

Wow, indeed. The kiss had been...well, wow. She hesitated for a moment, then tried to speak. "I do—" She cleared her throat, then continued, her voice tentative but steady. "I don't think we should do this."

His gaze sharpened, making her pulse race. "We shouldn't? Why not? We're both grown adults, not attached." Then his expression flickered with doubt. "Right?"

That comment sparked a fiery recollection of the woman with Pup, and her anger flared through her veins. "You have room to talk. You already have someone." She threw her hands up in exasperation. "I can't believe you kissed me when you have a girlfriend."

He paused, taken aback. "Whoa, whoa! What is this crazy talk? I don't have a girlfriend."

Elena's brow furrowed, her confidence wavering. Was he just spinning lies to get her into his bed? The suspicion lingered, shadowing her thoughts. "The woman with you the night you came to my apartment." She recalled the subtle way he had smiled when she called him.

Pup chuckled, breaking the moment. "That was my sister, Maria."

Elena's cheeks heated with embarrassment. She hadn't even considered that he might have siblings. Her jealousy—and she admitted, a twinge of it so early in their relationship—had blinded her to that possibility. Now, with a clearer view, she saw the chemistry between them was unmistakable. Still, she was his boss, and that complicated everything.

While Elena's thoughts spun in a whirl, Pup moved closer, gently but firmly guiding her backward until she was pressed against the wall. His hands found anchor on either side of her, the proximity firing her pulse and igniting a flush across her skin. The angry kid she'd met on their doorstep was gone, replaced by something darker, more predatory. She realized she was now his prey, and surprisingly, she found she liked the thrill.

Putting her hand on his chest—his rock-hard chest—she hesitated, her voice trembling slightly. "We really shouldn't do this."

He leaned in closer, his breath warm against her skin, a teasing smile playing on his lips. "Shouldn't? Again, why not?"

"Because." Her stomach fluttered with nerves. "I'm your boss."

Pup leaned back, raising an eyebrow with a hint of challenge. "Is that all?" His voice was smooth and teasing.

She gulped, her heart pounding, and nodded finally. "Yes."

"Then I quit."

His lips traced a passionate path down her throat, igniting a fiery tension between them. Elena's breath hitched, her longing roaring through her with every touch of his lips. "You can't quit."

Leaning back, he grinned, eyes dark with temptation. "How about we forget until daylight breaks? I intend to savor every moment and forget about work altogether."

Elena's heart raced as she yearned to pull him closer, the tantalizing distance between them electrifying. She couldn't speak, could barely breathe. Then, his lips touched hers.

His warm, strong lips claimed hers in a passionate kiss that sparked a fire through her core. His tongue danced into her eager mouth, devouring every offering she made, leaving her craving more. With her heart pounding in her ears, she barely registered her moan of pleasure. What was it about this kid—no, man, that could leave her so breathless? Her ex never had this effect on her. She stiffened slightly at the comparison.

Pup gently broke the kiss, concern flickering in his eyes. "What? What were you just thinking?"

Caught off guard and frustrated with herself for ruining the moment, she shook her head, a shy smile playing on her lips. "Nothing." Her cheeks warmed.

Not one to turn away from what she truly desired, she gently but firmly grasped a handful of his shirt and pulled him closer. Her voice was soft but compelling. "Kiss me again."

Pup's eyes lit up, and her heart skipped a beat at the sight. He gave her a playful smile. "Sure thing, Patience."

She wondered about the Patience comment, but before she could think again, his lips were on hers, hot, wet, and demanding. With her legs weakening, she nearly collapsed in his arms.

Pup broke the kiss and placed his forehead on hers. "Damn, you taste good." His finger traced a line on her jaw. "I bet you taste good everywhere."

Flame licked in her core at the thought of him tasting her everywhere. "Shut up and kiss me."

Pup chuckled, but his lips were quickly on hers, taking all she offered.

Things escalated rapidly from there.

Their kiss ignited a frenzy, hands fumbling urgently to shed each other's clothes, pausing only to toss off their shirts.

She worked on unbuttoning his jeans, but he gently pushed her away and stepped back. "Shoes."

Frustration flared. Why had she chosen her combat boots, just like his, when they were staying in? It stole precious moments from the electric connection of their lips.

They settled on the couch, each kicking off their boots, then rose to remove their jeans.

"Bedroom." Pup's growl held a commanding tone. He seized her hand, leading her to her room, now occupied by Tiki.

As they stepped into the room, he pulled her close, his eyes locked on hers. "I need to taste you again." His voice was a low, enticing promise before capturing her lips in a kiss that burned with intensity.

When they finally broke apart for air, Elena turned to Tiki. "Tiki, Geh Raus!" Tiki obeyed, leaping off the bed and exiting the room with a wag of her tail.

Pup chuckled softly, and Elena couldn't suppress a smile, realizing she might have accidentally sent Tiki on an adventure, despite her mastery of German commands. "What did I just say?" Her grin widened.

As he spun her around, he deftly unclasped her bra. "You sent her outside. I hope she doesn't know how to open doors on her own."

A wave of embarrassment washed over Elena, and she felt her cheeks flush. "I can't believe I said that." She laughed, her heart racing with a mix of amusement and anticipation.

As Pup gently slipped her bra off her shoulders, he pulled her close, his bare chest a vivid reminder of their intense, whirlwind kisses and touch. Though she hadn't yet had the chance to explore the contours of his muscles, her mind was already racing with anticipation, eager to trace every line and curve once she turned back around.

With his rigid cock against her, she momentarily lost her breath. This was a moment she couldn't resist, and she boldly set aside any rules HIS had.

Her desire was undeniable. As Pup had put it, "They were grown adults." Besides, who would ever know the true story of their trip? Unless Pup chose to spill the beans —and she had a hunch he'd keep it under wraps, just like she would.

After he gently traced a passionate kiss down her back, she turned to face him, her inhibitions melting away. With him, there was no embarrassment, only an exhilarating sense of the moment's importance. They were on the brink of a sexual connection, ready to satisfy the yearning within her for the man who had transformed from a mere annoyance to someone she craved with every fiber of her being.

"All's fair—" she began, reaching for his underwear.

He was there first. "In love and war. And, baby, that's what we've got."

She couldn't deny it was true, but now wasn't the time to discuss it. "Mhm." Her eyes were fixed on him as he pulled down his underwear, revealing his rigid erection.

"Honey, one of us has too many clothes on."

After admiring his hard length, Elena slipped away from his grasp and climbed onto the bed, settling in the middle on her knees. She quietly patted the space next to her. "Come here." She wasn't intending to be sultry, but her voice certainly had that effect.

"Honey, a pack of adorable puppies couldn't keep me from you." He climbed onto the bed and sat next to her.

Elena chuckled. Although it wasn't the most conventional line, it perfectly encapsulated his personality.

"Oh, I'm quite the comedian, am I?"

As she giggled more, he reached over and pulled her onto his lap, quickly lying back so she was on top of him.

She sobered, her gaze fixed on his lust-filled amber eyes. "Oh."

With his hard cock pressed against her core, the fiery inferno inside her erupted in all directions, engulfing her body and making her feel as if she couldn't bear the intense heat. *And this is only the beginning.*

"Elena, you can't keep those panties on for what's about to happen."

The fact that he hadn't taken advantage of her vulnerability spoke volumes about his character. He was giving her the freedom to decide, even at this critical juncture. That act endeared him to her even more. "I know." Then she smiled in what she hoped was her most mischievous smile. "After I finish exploring."

His eyes lit up with excitement, and he couldn't help but smile. He gently removed his arms from around her and laid them on the bed. "Go ahead. Don't be shy."

She smiled back, appreciating his cuteness. "Oh, I plan to." She bravely claimed his mouth, savoring the warmth of him, until stars burst behind her eyes.

He moaned, and she realized she would have the entire night to play—but not their first time. So, she broke the kiss and smiled as he groaned in response. She trailed kisses on his neck, just like he had done to her, and then moved to his ear, sucking on his lobe, all the while keeping her core moving slowly over his erection.

"Mm."

Releasing his earlobe, she licked her way down his neck, savoring the sensation. She had never been one for shaved chests, but she found the lack of hair while loving his chest quite pleasant.

She focused on his right nipple, and Pup groaned when she sucked on it. She loved her nipples to be teased, but she knew it wasn't the same as loving the rest of his body—the intimate parts. So, she didn't linger. Her hand led her tongue down a path on his stomach, where he was also…shaved.

Wow. She had never been with a man who took such care of his body. At that moment, she decided that all her men should be shaved. The thought of it made her feel a sour sensation in her stomach, and she couldn't understand why. Maybe it was the thought of other men after this. That couldn't be it, she decided.

"Everything okay?" Pup looked at her with a smile.

Realizing she had stopped in her thought process, she smiled back. "Of course. I've never been with a man who is so manscaped, I believe they call it."

A blush spread across his cheeks, and she found it endearing. "Well, I—"

"No. I like it."

"Oh, well then, carry on."

"Aren't I the one who would typically issue those commands?"

"No work." He groaned, dropping his head back onto the bed. "No work."

He was right. Her teasing had been wrong because it reminded her that this was unacceptable. However, as she gazed upon his erect cock, and her hand descended to grasp it, she no longer cared. "You're right."

Allowing her libido to guide her, she skillfully slid her hand up and down his cock. As Pup's body tensed, she teased the head with her tongue, sending him nearly flying off the bed.

He grabbed the covers with his hands. "Damn."

Watching him as she slowly descended her mouth on him, she moaned in pleasure. The intense heat between them made her realize that he was holding back on her account.

Yet, she had never been one to be the aggressor in bed. She had always been more passive, allowing the guy to take the lead.

This newfound strength in her was...heady.

She sucked her way back up his cock and lifted her lips with a pop. "I like this." She hadn't been able to take him fully into her mouth, so her hand remained around the base of his dick.

"I do, too." He groaned. "I do, too."

Catching his gaze, watching her, she kept her eyes on him as she continued up and down his length. It wasn't long before Pup reached for her. "Enough."

Elena laughed and playfully pulled out of his reach before landing on the bed next to him. He quickly outstretched his hand for her panties, and she didn't stop him.

"These must go." He pulled them down the legs, and she was glad she'd shaved that morning.

She couldn't agree more. It was time.

Chapter Nineteen

Pup lounged on the bed, captivated by Elena's radiant presence. Her beauty was undeniable, and he had always suspected she concealed something extraordinary beneath her tough exterior. Yet, nothing could have prepared him for the breathtaking perfection she revealed.

"Turnabout is fair play." He grinned mischievously.

Elena's smile widened, her eyes alight with anticipation, as the fire within him roared to life. "It is."

Lying down, he gently traced his hand over her chest, circling her breasts with a teasing touch before guiding it down her stomach to her core. "I can't wait to taste you here." His voice was a low, enticing whisper of promise.

Her body responded with a soft moan. "I dare you."

He raised an eyebrow, intrigued. "Oh really?" He slipped one finger inside her, then withdrew it. He brought it to his lips, savoring the taste. "Perfection." He captured her mouth, their lips meeting with the lingering essence of her taste.

Their lips locked in a passionate embrace, tongues entwined in a sensual dance, and he gently caressed her breast. With a tender touch, he teased her nipple, eliciting a soft moan that sent a surge of desire coursing through him. Though his dick urged him to skip the foreplay, he knew better. He was committed to pleasing her like no other, a thought that momentarily paused him, leaving him puzzled.

Shaking off the distraction, he broke the kiss and continued his journey, trailing kisses down her chest to her breast.

As he gently caressed her breast with his tongue, his other hand playfully teased her other nipple. When he took her nipple into his mouth and began to suck, she clutched the cover and arched her back in response. He mentally noted the sensitivity of her breasts, eager to explore further.

She gently took hold of his face, lifting it until their eyes locked in a moment of intense connection. "I'll make you a deal. If you indulge me now, I'll allow you to fully explore me later tonight."

Pup had always known Elena to be formidable, but he never anticipated such strength in the bedroom. Most women he had encountered were either timid or excessively strong, even for him. Elena stood out as the perfect balance.

A smile tugged at the corners of his mouth as he imagined her utter perfection. "I don't know. I remember a challenge."

Her face turned a deeper shade of crimson, and he couldn't help but chuckle at her cuteness. "I take it back." She shook her head. "No, I don't, but not now, later."

Pup glanced down her stomach at the patch of hair

and then back at her. "I don't know. I'm quite looking forward to it."

"Please."

Definitely "Patience." Taking only a moment to consider her offer, he rolled off the bed.

"Where are you going?" Her voice trembled with apprehension.

"Just to get a condom."

"You brought condoms on an op?"

He smiled, left the room, and then returned with several packages from his bag. He deposited the extra condoms on the bedside table, then opened one and rolled it on. "Honey, I'm never caught off guard."

She snorted at that, but he caught her secret smile. Oh, yeah, she enjoyed his wit.

"What?" He crawled onto the bed. "You didn't bring them with you?"

Elena shook her head and bit her lip. "Do you have enough for tonight?"

Pup's grin widened. "And then some."

She laughed as he lay beside her.

After a moment, they fell silent, their eyes locked in a gaze.

"Are you certain you're okay with this?"

She nodded slowly. "I am."

"Well, then, let's get this show on the road."

"I thought we'd already begun."

His adrenaline surged at the memory of her lips on his dick. At the thought, said dick decided to twitch, reminding him of his need. He wanted to explore her body, but he knew he would have to wait. Now, he had to have her.

Sliding his hand down her body, he tested the waters. "Wow, you're ready for me, aren't you?"

A wide smile spread across her face. "You could say that."

Slowly, he climbed atop her, ensuring his weight didn't press against her. Reaching down, he positioned his cock at her entrance and slowly pushed in. The warm sensation enveloped his tip, and he eagerly anticipated more, but he wouldn't rush the process. Considering she wasn't likely a virgin, she was surprisingly snug for him. Although he wasn't huge, he was aware of his girth, which some women might find uncomfortable. He hoped she could tolerate it.

When he withdrew and pushed in more, biting his tongue to avoid thrusting into her with all his might. He would take this slowly until she was accustomed to him, as he didn't want to ruin the night immediately.

Again, he groaned against the slow pace of pushing into her. Then, she pulled her legs up and wrapped them around his waist, her heels digging in to encourage him. With one last breath, he thrust into her.

She moaned, and he remained still, hesitant to take another breath before ensuring she was okay.

"Breathe." Her voice in his ear filled with reassurance, comforted him. "I'm fine."

He pulled back and gazed upon her. Her face flushed, and she radiated an ethereal beauty that left him spellbound.

Slowly, he withdrew slightly and pushed into her again, all the while watching her enormous eyes change as desire overtook them. Knowing he was the cause of it, the feel of it left him enraptured.

"More." She took her mouth in a kiss that imprinted on his soul. This woman did something wonderful to him with her olive skin, mesmerizing chocolate brown eyes, and perfect body. He feared tonight might not be enough, but he knew that was all she'd ever agree to with him.

Pup pushed that dark thought aside as he rocked in and out of her, each thrust more heavenly than the last.

Breaking the kiss, he rested his forehead against hers as beads of sweat began to appear on their bodies from the exertion. He wouldn't be rushed this first time.

"This is—" He trailed off, unsure of how to complete the thought. Perfection? He had already seen her that way, so why not this moment too?

"Mm." She closed her eyes and gently rubbed her feet up and down his back, creating the perfect angle to deepen their connection.

It was a challenge to hold back, but he sensed she wasn't quite ready, so he maintained the rhythm that was drawing him closer, hoping it would do the same for her.

When he felt the tingling at the base of his spine, he rocked into her again and captured her nipple with his tongue and teeth.

"Pup."

He pulled his head back and looked at her closed eyes. "My name is Kevin." He wasn't sure why he corrected her. Then he knew. This wasn't work. He wasn't Pup. He was Kevin, and she was Elena. He wanted to hear her acknowledge that.

She opened those beautiful eyes and smiled.

"Kevin."

That did it. It was time to move this forward. He reached between them, rubbing her clit while his mouth moved back to her breast, and his cock entered and withdrew, almost putting him over the edge. She felt like heaven, and he was wearing a raincoat. Oh, how he'd love to enter her bareback at least once. But that was a dream he'd have to squelch.

Elena moaned, and he sensed her imminent orgasm as her body arched off the bed when he intensified his pressure on her clit.

He intended to make her come more than once tonight, but he couldn't handle more than once this first time. He had been drawn to her longer than he had realized, and he couldn't resist.

Her breath came in pants, and the glistening of sweat intensified, a testament to their intense efforts to please each other.

Her hands gently ran through his short hair and against the nearly shaved sides. "I'm close."

Thank the fuck for that reassurance, because he was clinging by a thread. "Come on, honey, let go."

He pushed in deeper, hoping not to hurt her. They had ample time to explore and enjoy each other's company, and he didn't want to ruin it immediately.

The tingling at the base of his spine intensified, and he was close. Too close.

"Oh, Kevin."

Elena's sudden and intense response sent him over the edge without another movement. Waves of pleasure crashed over him, overwhelming him with ecstasy, stronger than he'd ever felt. He was limp and exhausted. This was the first time he had experienced an orgasm at the same time as the woman in his bed, and he knew that he wanted to repeat it again and again...with Elena.

Sated, he withdrew and rolled off her, lying flat on his back to catch his breath. "That was incredible."

"Yeah. That was quite...hot."

Hot definitely described their first encounter. Now, however, it was playtime, and he eagerly anticipated every moment. Slipping off the bed, he made his way to the bathroom to dispose of the used condom.

She laughed as he approached the nightstand and grabbed another condom. He was already getting hard again, and tasting her was sure to fuel his erection. But they needed a quick breather to restore the energy they'd expended.

"You really meant all night, didn't you?"

Pup nodded as he settled onto the bed. "I did. I think we should have a late-night snack to keep our energy up, and then we can sleep on the flight."

Elena gently ran her hands up and down his chest, stirring him even more. "You've got it all figured out."

"As I said, I'm never caught off guard."

"Right. I forgot that."

A pounding at the door sent Pup straight off the bed and on alert. "Did you order anything?" He rushed to pull on his cargo pants.

"No." Elena scurried off the bed, looking for her clothing and slipping into her jeans commando.

He groaned at that until the knock sounded again.

When Pup opened the bedroom door, the dogs were

sitting near the hotel door, whining. However, they weren't barking, which made him feel better. He wasn't aware of Tiki's behaviors, but if someone he deemed a threat—in any way—Casey would bark at them.

"Hey, guys, it's Daylan and Buddy."

That's why the dogs whined. They recognized Buddy. But what the fuck was this guy doing here?

For the first time, Pup was caught off guard.

Pup wrenched open the door and narrowed his eyes at Daylan. "What the hell are you doing here?"

"Our flight home was canceled, and Emily rescheduled me with you guys for tomorrow. Would it be okay if we crashed? She mentioned that you had a pullout sofa."

Pup was about to respond when he turned to Elena, who looked shocked. He didn't want their night together to end, but what could he say? This was a teammate, and he couldn't just kick him out. Or could he?

Pup turned back to Daylan. "Come on in." He moved aside to let the agent and K9 enter. Sure, the hotel would be upset about three dogs in a room without their permission, but he didn't care. Now, he had damage control to handle because Daylan's nose was already active, and his eyes widened in surprise as he noticed Pup's shirtless state and Elena's haphazard attempt at dressing.

Hell, the entire place, including them, smelled like sex. There was no getting around it.

Daylan paused just inside the door. "Look, if I'm interrupting."

Pup was about to respond when Elena stepped

forward. "Of course you're not."

His ire intensified at her sudden shift from wanting the night with him to dismissing Daylan's interference. He wouldn't have been so benevolent.

Daylan glanced at Pup, who shrugged in response. "The couch does pull out." He turned to Elena and stormed off to his room for a shirt. He couldn't go to Elena's—which Daylan would find out when they went to sleep—and confirm things for Daylan.

As he turned, he noticed the dogs sniffing each other's butts, while Casey attempted to play with the older dogs. However, they had more training and wouldn't play until allowed, which Pup found frustrating for the young K9.

After donning a shirt, he returned to the outer room, and he instinctively turned to the two who were engrossed in a hushed conversation. A chill ran down his spine as he wondered what they could be discussing. Was it the fact that Daylan had realized they'd been sleeping together? Was he scolding her about the policy? Or was she desperately trying to explain it away? Whatever it was, it didn't sit right with him because it wasn't Daylan's business.

He approached them. "So, Daylan, what brings you to this part of California?"

The two separated, and only Elena appeared embarrassed by their conversation. Was she already regretting their interaction? Well, he had news for her. She owed him a night, and he would find a way to make it happen.

"Just a layover. Have you eaten? I'm starving."

Pup wanted to ask him if he had lost his damn mind. The full food cart sat nearby, so he lied. "Yeah."

Elena smiled sweetly, and her words kicked him in the gut. "I'd love some dessert."

"So would I." But he wasn't referring to a dessert filled with sugar.

Daylan raised his eyebrows. "What?"

"Oh, nothing. Dessert sounds fine."

Elena took everyone's dessert order and phoned it into room service, while Pup wheeled the full cart into the hallway. He hated to see the waste, but they needed a cover story.

After ending the call, she turned to the men. "TV, then? I believe sports is on one of these channels."

Pup wondered if Elena enjoyed sports or was simply trying to steer the conversation away from the two of them.

"I think I'll walk Tiki." Elena handed the remote to Daylan.

Pup jumped on that. "I think Casey needs to go out for the night, too."

Elena raised her hand to stop him. "I can take them both."

So, that's how it would go. She would avoid him. Well, she could have the night, but she couldn't run tomorrow. She sat beside him on the plane. Their dogs could have the adjoining seats while they sat together. Then, they'd talk it out.

Having figured it all out, he let her have this win. "Thanks." Yes, he'd let her have this win because tomorrow, he was waging an all-out war on her mind and body.

Chapter Twenty

Pup couldn't believe his eyes. Elena nestled Tiki into the seat beside her, instead of across with Casey as Pup had expected. "How about we sit the dogs together?" He was already making his way to buckle Casey's harness into the window seat.

But Elena shook her head. "No, I think we should each sit with them since this is a commercial flight."

Daylan lurked behind them. "She's probably right."

Pup's stomach clenched. Son of a bitch—he really didn't like Daylan. The guy kept popping up at the worst moments. Thanks to Emily, Daylan was booked in first class with them, making the man's unexpected presence feel all the more intrusive.

So, they each sat in first class on the flight, a dog nestled beside them. Elena claimed the window seat, cutting him off from any chance to talk across the aisle. Meanwhile, Daylan sat behind her, and Pup caught whispers of their secret conversations through the crack between their seats that fluttered through the cabin. His fists clenched. He ached to crush something. Maybe head to that new club where they specialize in one thing—

smashing and releasing rage.

But he knew he shouldn't be angry. Crossing the line from friends to lovers was a mistake they shouldn't have made, yet they did it anyway. He'd promised her that come daylight, they'd revert to normal. But now, it seemed Elena planned to avoid him altogether. How would that even work, especially with her as his boss? The tension was thick, and he couldn't shake the gnawing worry about the future.

Pup must have dozed off because when he woke up, the flight attendant was instructing him to bring his seat upright for landing. Looking down, he noticed Casey sleeping on his lap, and the center armrest lowered. When had he done that? He was glad he had done so because his dog could get comfortable. Then he remembered, not his dog. Could the day get any worse?

After landing and deplaning, they went to the luggage claim for the empty kennels and their baggage. The dogs were so well-behaved that they generally didn't need a kennel, but sometimes, a client preferred the dog crated.

He regretted that he and Elena hadn't ridden together to the airport, but he had had a side errand to run, so they'd each taken their vehicles. Dropping off money for his sister had been a necessity as she'd just been laid off, and rent was due. He knew she'd find something fast, but he wouldn't allow her bills to suffer in the meantime.

Now, Elena was giving Daylan a ride because he had a friend drop him off at the airport. Why couldn't he call that same friend now?

Pup could sense the man moving in on Elena. Did he

think she was easy because she had slept with him? He would have to set the man straight if that was the case.

As they parted ways in the parking lot, Elena turned to him. "See you bright and early at 0700 at the kennels."

She would see him sooner than that. They resided in the same building, and they would have a chat tonight. He nodded in agreement to the time and turned away, leaving the others in his wake as he almost stomped off like a petulant child to his truck.

Why was he so angry? Was it at Elena, or maybe at himself? Perhaps a little at Daylan, but mostly at himself. He'd allowed himself to become deeply invested in Elena and their night together. Losing control over his emotions tugged painfully at his heartstrings, leaving him confused. That's what fueled his anger—the reaction of a passionate lover, not a colleague who had a casual encounter.

He carefully settled Casey into the seat beside him, securing her harness with practiced precision before starting his truck. He sat there, lost in thought, trying to sort through a tangled mess of emotions. He chuckled softly to himself—no pun intended—feeling more like a reckless young pup than a steady man. Clearly, settling down was the priority now.

Just as he was about to shift into gear, a sharp tap on the door jolted him. He nearly reached for the weapon he kept concealed in the door panel.

Daylan's voice came steady but unmistakable. "Pup."

He stiffened, irritation flickering. What the hell did the fucker want now? "What?" He rolled down the window.

Daylan raised an eyebrow but didn't comment on Pup's tone. "Elena's got four flat tires."

Stunned, Pup frantically jabbed the button to shut off the truck. "Which way?" As if he hadn't noticed Elena's vehicle parked nearby when he arrived at the airport lot before they'd left on this fucked up op.

Daylan pointed. "I'll show you."

Pup nodded, gently released Casey's harness, and hopped out. "Come on, girl. Looks like you'll meet the others sooner than expected!"

When they reached Elena's car, they found her pacing anxiously, talking rapidly in Spanish on the phone. The vehicle was running, with the dogs inside, probably kept warm. Pup opened the back door, and Casey eagerly joined the others, sitting patiently as they watched Elena.

"What happened?" Pup narrowed his eyes at a slash in one of the tires. A rock hit his gut with a splash. This was intentional.

"Someone slashed all four."

"And airport security did nothing?"

Daylan shrugged, a hint of frustration in his tone. "How would I know?" Then he turned, sighing heavily. "But look, here they are now."

Sure enough, airport security pulled up behind Elena, blocking her in. She wasn't about to drive off with four flat tires.

Pup turned to Daylan. "Did you call it in?"

Daylan nodded, raising his phone. "Talked to Devon."

The air was thick with anticipation as they watched the security team draw nearer. The guard stepped forward, extending a hand to Daylan. Why him? Was it because Daylan was towering at six feet three, while he was only five-eleven? He really needed to get past the height thing, but experience had shown him that tall men often gravitated toward others of similar stature when they greeted.

The security officer smiled. "I'm Wyatt. We spotted this problem earlier today, around four a.m. I just got a call—on my way here—that it was one of HIS's agents. We're truly sorry about that."

Elena stepped closer, her phone now at her side. "And you should be." She reached up, pinching the bridge of her nose before releasing it. "I'm sorry. It's not your fault. But tell me—what about the cameras?"

"You can come and see them, but unfortunately, we didn't catch anything. This is at the edge of the camera's view, and the large SUV beside you blocked most of the view. We did manage to spot a truck leaving, but unfortunately, we couldn't see its license plate."

Who was that person who was so angry with Elena that they would do that? Who knew she was leaving? It had been a spontaneous operation. It may have been a crime of opportunity, but all four tires. Pup didn't believe it. "We'll review the tapes."

Elena tensed beside him. Then, she relaxed. "Yes, let's review the tapes. I've already called a tow truck, so someone needs to stay with the vehicle and the dogs."

Daylan, bless his black heart, stepped forward. "I'll take care of it." He turned to Pup. "If you're not back when the tow truck arrives, can I bring them to your truck?"

As long as he wasn't accompanying them inside the airport, Pup would gladly give him the truck itself. "Of course." He reached into his pocket and tossed the key fob to Daylan.

Knowing the dogs would get anxious if left alone, he calmly opened the door and told Casey, "Bleib," the command to stay.

Daylan chuckled. "And she'll stay right there when the tow truck arrives."

Pup rolled his eyes. "You'll figure it out." Then, he focused, turning to Elena. "You ready?"

She nodded confidently, and together they followed Wyatt to his security truck.

They crammed into the front seat, Elena wedged between them, and Wyatt must have felt the tension between them because the air was thick with it.

Airport security's setup was questionable at best. Anyone could overpower the officer. Pup's mind raced, feeling both empathy and frustration. He knew all too well the struggles of underfunded security teams, living on tight government budgets. The memory of lacking necessities while a U.S. deputy marshal sent a shiver down his spine, fueling his resolve to find out who did this to Elena's vehicle.

Once inside the airport security office, they encountered two more officers, Bryan and Hagan, who were just about to depart. Steve, the man monitoring the security cameras, turned to face them with a sharp look. "Yeah, we couldn't catch the plate—or even tell if there was one. If there was, it was covered by a blackout cover." His eyes flicked between Elena and him. "Did you know they were illegal?"

Pup, unfazed by the question, simply wanted to figure out who might pose a threat to Elena. If these suspects were capable of such a stunt, things could get worse. And Pup wasn't about to let that happen.

He didn't question his instinct to protect Elena. She was, after all, another agent, and he'd step up for any of them in danger. Yet, he couldn't shake the guilt, knowing he'd usually expect agents to fend for themselves while he backed them up, not that he'd step up front.

Internally, he sighed. That's what happened when you blurred the lines between work and...well, another kind of work—a more enjoyable one.

Elena smiled. "I did hear that. Now, about the video feed?"

"Oh, sure." Steve turned to the keyboard and mouse. "Give me a minute."

Pup watched as Steve navigated through the footage, stopping at a moment when a truck approached Elena's vehicle. "Stop."

Steve looked back, as if he'd already anticipated the command. "Here we go."

Elena leaned in, her eyes narrowing and jaw tightening as she watched the footage. She recognized the truck or perhaps the person whose face was obscured.

Pup eagerly waited for her to say, "I know who that is," but instead, she just shook her head softly. When she didn't ask to watch it again, he immediately understood—she'd recognized something but didn't need to confirm it. Respecting her silence, he quietly thanked the security team.

Elena took copies of the report for her insurance, and the trio drove back to Pup's truck, where the three dogs were curled up in the front and back seats.

Wyatt left them in the cold, Pup still wondering who would do this to Elena.

Daylan nodded toward the airport. "Anything?"

Elena shook her head once more. "No." With her expression unreadable, her quiet demeanor spoke volumes.

Pup pushed to call her out, but hesitated, deciding to wait until they were alone.

Daylan flicked his thumb over his shoulder toward a car and the attractive female driver.

Pup nodded, offering a casual hand. "See ya, man."

Daylan returned the nod, reaching out to grasp Pup's hand. "I'll just grab Buddy and hit the road." Then he looked at Elena, a hint of concern in his voice. "Need a ride? We can squeeze you in."

Pup surprised himself. "That's okay, I've got her." Elena's tense back told him she might want to protest, but with all the crates—broken down or not—the tiny car wouldn't hold everyone anyway.

Daylan raised his brows, arching an inquisitive look at her. "Elena?" His tone was subtle yet curious.

Pup bristled at the thought of someone questioning him. He was tempted to step up and punch the guy in the face for even suggesting doubt. But part of him still trusted Daylan's concern for Elena as another agent. Conflicting feelings swirled inside him.

Elena waved a dismissive hand. "It's fine. We live in the same building, so it makes sense. Besides, we'd never fit in the car with the dogs, crates, and luggage."

Daylan nodded. "Okay, see you at 0700." He opened the truck door. Buddy, eager and energetic, bounded out instantly, sticking close to Daylan, craving attention.

"Let's go, Buddy."

Watching Daylan settle the K9 into the vehicle and the agent hop in, Pup braced for a lecture from her about taking charge of her ride home or for her to criticize his interference in what she considered "her" problem. But she was mistaken. One agent's problem was everyone's.

He turned to Elena, the woman who constantly baffled him. "Let's get the dogs settled in the back seat." His large cab with a smaller backseat seemed perfect for Casey when another agent rode along. But to someone else, it might feel cramped. Maybe he should've gone with the king cab.

He wasn't sure why his usual confidence in his mode of transportation suddenly waned. It had never happened before. But today was different. He was behind the wheel for her, his "boss," in full boss mode.

Once they were settled and buckled up, he started the truck, then leaned his left arm over the steering wheel and glanced over at her. "Who was it?" He knew she understood without needing to explain.

She looked ahead, a sigh escaping her lips. "It's a truck we used during SWAT training exercises."

The weight of her words hung in the air, making the moment tense yet charged with unspoken stakes.

Chapter Twenty-One

Things only got worse for Elena after finding out her tires had been slashed. She had to spend the time rambling on about future K9 training to keep Pup from bringing up "the event" as she'd dubbed it. Wow, she should be calling him Kevin, considering how close they'd gotten, but by gosh, that would give everything away and make it more personal. Like when I'd called him Kevin in the heat of the moment.

And it wasn't more personal. Professionalism was the only way to keep their relationship. Wasn't it?

"Are we going to talk about it?"

Her breath caught. "No."

"Uh-huh. Okay, well then, continue on."

Jerk. He knew she was prattling on to avoid talking about their time together. But she had no choice.

Thankfully, the traffic was surprisingly light as they made their way to Baltimore's Inner Harbor, where their apartment building stood.

As they pulled into the parking lot, Elena's heart skipped a beat. There, on their doorstep, sat her team leader. Trouble had definitely found her.

She never intended for him to cut his vacation short just for her, nor did she want him rushing to her side over a mere four slashed tires. She could more than handle her SWAT buddies on her own. His backup wasn't needed. The men had no clue of the storm they were about to face.

Pup nodded to the front of the building. "Boss is here."

As soon as the truck came to a halt, she was already unbuckling her seatbelt, eager to leap out. After releasing Tiki's seatbelt, she led the dog out of the truck, and together they made their way to the grassy area near the building. Boss could wait. The dog was her priority, and he knew it.

Pup followed behind her, and she couldn't fault him for it. The airport was a bustling maze with no designated spot for dogs. But during their layover, she discovered a delightful surprise. They had a "pet area" complete with lush, inviting grass. It was a haven for pets to stretch their legs and relieve themselves before and after enduring long flights. She had never heard of such a thoughtful amenity before and fervently hoped it would become a trend at airports everywhere.

"I'll handle the luggage. Once I've settled Casey in."

Grateful to finally free Boss's wait, she nodded. "Thanks."

Pup dismissed her thanks with a wave. "No trouble at all."

She could sense his curiosity about the impending conversation between her and her boss. She hesitated, unsure if she wanted him—or even herself to hear what was about to unfold.

As they approached, Boss stood tall, his presence commanding attention. He nodded with a knowing smile. "Elena. Pup." With a gentle gesture, he leaned down, inviting Tiki to sniff his hand. "Remember me, girl?" After a few affectionate pats for Tiki, he extended his hand to Casey, sharing the same kindness.

Pup's curiosity won out. "Whatcha here for?"

Boss straightened, his expression serious. "We got a call from your landlord. There's a problem with your apartment. I—"

With Elena's mind elsewhere, she frantically searched for her keys in her purse. Pup, faster than her, unlocked the door with ease. He stepped aside, letting her enter first. Her heart raced as she dashed down the hall, only to be met by the ominous sight of police tape across her door.

How much more fucked up could this day get?

Ignoring the law, she tore the tape off and unlocked her door with the keys she had finally managed to retrieve. Her pulse raced with anticipation of what horrors might lie within.

A pit formed in her stomach as she took in the devastation. Her belongings were in ruins. Furniture was shredded and overturned, papers scattered around the desk. She sprinted to her bedroom, only to find her mattress slashed open, stuffing spilling everywhere. Her clothes were strewn about, their condition unknown, but she suspected they were beyond repair.

Mark. That was the name that flashed through her mind as the culprit behind this vile act because it was his style. It had to be him. SWAT would've staged something more dramatic, like planting a body or evidence, not simply vandalizing her home.

They had slashed her tires, a juvenile act that just angered her more and cost her money.

Pup whistled softly behind her, breaking the silence. "Elena, I'll take Tiki to my apartment."

Elena could only nod, her eyes fixed on the wreckage before her. The murmurs between Pup and Boss drifted past her, but she was too overwhelmed to care. Her world felt like it was crumbling.

Boss stepped beside her. "Elena, we'll figure this out. You've got all of us behind you."

Slowly, she turned to face him. "This can't be happening to me."

She found herself caught in a whirlwind of chaos, with two adversaries determined to ruin her life, and they had done just that. Her precious savings were now destined for tires, and it seemed like clothing, furniture, and household goods would soon follow. It was a daunting task to rebuild what she had lost. Mark was aware of this, hoping she would come crawling back, admitting defeat. But wait—hadn't Luis said that he accused her of being responsible for his arrest? Could this outburst be his way of seeking revenge?

"Let's head to Pup's apartment and have a chat."

"No." Elena shook her head. "I need to handle this myself."

"The teams are on their way to assist." She knew he was right, but it didn't ease her mind.

"I don't want strangers rummaging through my belongings." And she meant it. Especially her clothes, where her most intimate items were kept. She wasn't overly modest, but the thought of an unfamiliar man touching her underwear felt unsettling.

"They'll only help with the larger items and cleanup. We'll leave your clothes and paperwork untouched."

She hadn't even thought about her paperwork until now. Her heart hammered as she dashed to her now-empty file cabinet, dropping to her knees and frantically sifting through the scattered papers on the floor. "It has to be here. It has to."

"Elena, what's going on? Can I help?"

"No." The initial pit in her stomach swirled into a whirlwind of distress. "It has to be here. It has to."

Boss knelt beside her, gently stopping her hands. "Elena. Look at me."

"It has to be here." She met his gaze.

"I need you to calm down and tell me what has to be here."

Realizing there was no time to delay the chaos in her life, she sat back on her haunches. "The lawsuit paperwork against the SWAT team for sexual harassment."

Boss whistled, neither criticizing her for suing her former teammates nor doubting the validity of her claim. Instead, he nodded. "Okay. Let's look."

As they sifted through the papers, they piled them up in a chaotic jumble. She was relieved that Boss refrained from peeking into her financial or personal details, simply tossing them aside into a stack that didn't contain the crucial legal documents she was searching for.

But they were nowhere to be found. The lawsuit

hadn't been filed yet. She only had the preliminary paperwork, and now Mark had it. While it wouldn't prevent her attorney from filing the case in the coming days, it did give SWAT an unwelcome heads-up if Mark shared. Which, she suspected, he would.

Frustration boiled over. That's why they'd slashed her tires. Mark had already wreaked havoc on everything else. She was certain the mechanic would discover sugar in her gas tank once he inspected her SUV because they wanted her life in utter ruin.

A sense of relief washed over her—at least there hadn't been a bomb in her car. Yet, the thought sent a shiver down her spine. Why would they escalate from attempted murder to what felt like childish vandalism? The dread deepened, leaving her questioning what darkness she was truly up against.

Tears threatened to spill over, but she steeled herself. "It's not here."

Boss settled back, his expression thoughtful. "It doesn't seem like it. How about we head next door, grab a drink, and sort this out?" He paused, waiting for her to rise, a gesture she truly valued.

Yet, the thought of leaving this place and going to Pup's apartment was daunting. "Let's just stay here."

"No, let's go next door. You can't sit here. You need a break from this chaos." He was right. She needed to step away from the wreckage, even if just for a moment.

With a sigh, she nodded. "All right."

After they left, she locked her door and defiantly tore down the remaining police tape. Screw them. She knew she'd get a lecture for it later, but she didn't care right now.

As she approached Pup's apartment with a mix of fear and determination, she did what she always did when cornered. She strategized in her mind.

"Thank you, Boss." She stood at Pup's open door. Apparently, he'd been expecting them. She mentally shrugged it off.

"Don't mention it, Elena." He gestured for her to enter first, which she did. Inside, Pup was lounging on the couch, talking to dogs crammed into one large dog bed in the corner.

"I tossed in a blanket, but they were dead set on sharing the dog bed." Pup rose to his feet. His intense gaze locked onto hers, and she felt him probing her thoughts. First, the flat tires, then the vandalism. It was a whirlwind of a day for any girl.

"Thanks." Elena made her way to the dog bed. She crouched down to stroke Tiki, whose belly served as a cozy pillow for Casey's head. The bond between them was undeniable, and it unsettled her. She was determined to keep herself and Pup from spending too much time alone, which meant the dogs wouldn't either.

No, there would always be Daylan and Buddy during training sessions, or there wouldn't be any training at all. She'd concoct some explanation for the Hamilton brothers if they inquired, careful not to reveal that she'd slept with Pup on their first mission together.

Elena took a few deep breaths to steady her nerves, her heart skipping a beat at the tender look Pup gave her as she interacted with the dogs. It was undeniably... loving, and that only made her more uneasy.

She cleared her throat. "Thanks for letting us sit in here for a bit."

Pup narrowed his eyes, shaking his head. "No problem. Did you know that petting a dog can lower your blood pressure?"

Elena stared at him. Why always a "Did you know?" question? Of course, she knew all about dogs.

Boss observed them closely, then shook his head. "Let's sit."

Pup gestured towards the sofa and matching armchairs. "There's beer on the table if you'd like one."

"Thanks." Elena grabbed a beer and sank into an armchair. She preferred not to have Pup sitting next to her on the couch. The unspoken feeling between them was palpable, and she feared Boss might pick up on it.

Boss settled into the armchair with a confident air. "Now. Tell me about the explosion."

"Explosion?" Pup nearly yelped.

Amidst the chaos of today's events, the explosion had slipped her mind. She hadn't shared it with anyone except the brothers, so Pup was taken aback. This revelation reassured her that she could trust the family to keep her secrets. Yet, here was Boss, casually mentioning it in front of him.

Did it really matter if he knew? After all, he had risked everything by committing a crime for her, so she felt she owed him the full story.

The beer bottle glistened with condensation as it slid down her hand. "Well, Mark got arrested and then let go. I'm still in the dark about what's happening now."

"But they suspected you had an enemy, right?" Boss

inquired, taking a sip of his beer.

She nodded. "I'm not sure what tipped them off about Mark, but they figured he was in it for the money."

"What explosion?" Pup leaned forward with curiosity etched on his face. "Fill me in."

By the time she had filled Pup in on the explosion and Boss on the drugs, exhaustion had taken over. She longed for a long bath and a week-long sleep to escape into a new life, one free from toxic men.

Boss cleared his throat. "Where will you stay?"

"In my apartment." She momentarily forgot she had nowhere to sleep but the floor.

But Pup had a different idea. "Right here."

Their eyes met, and she knew there was no way she could stay in the same apartment with him. She remembered what had happened the last time they were in close proximity.

Before she could say "No," Boss stood up. "That's a perfect idea. You need someone watching your six right now, and this is ideal."

"But—"

Boss cut her off. "There's the team to help. Let's get moving."

What had just transpired? Was she being ordered to stay with Pup, or was it merely an option? It seemed like a foregone conclusion. How on earth was she going to escape this predicament?

Chapter Twenty-Two

Her teammates were nothing short of incredible. From her small team, there was the ever-reliable Doc, Cowboy, and Ballpark, while Bravo team boasted the formidable Grits, the sharp-witted Nemo, and the enigmatic Casper. Yet, a lingering question hung in the air. Who would step into the two vacant spots on Alpha team? It was a mystery how things had unfolded this way. She'd heard about Joe Stone's transition into tech with Devon, leaving a gap that was never filled, and then there was Sugar's departure, also without a replacement. Boss had finally declared it was high time to bolster their ranks once more. Whispers were circulating that a Russian team had once joined their ranks, but she hadn't confirmed it. It struck her as peculiar, yet she wasn't in the business of recruiting agents.

After the grueling cleanup, the group gathered in Pup's cozy apartment for some well-deserved fun. Boss and Grits had cleverly arranged for a delivery of beer, water, and wings to keep everyone's spirits high. As the aroma of sizzling wings filled the air, the crew eagerly took turns at the dartboard Pup had proudly displayed in the dining room, laughter echoing through the room.

Meanwhile, Elena chose to step back from the game, opting instead to sit with Boss and Grits to strategize their next moves. The agents had shown incredible generosity, offering up furniture, household items, and even a heartfelt bag of personal necessities, including cosmetic samples sent by their wives. Elena's eyes welled up with emotion as she opened it, touched by the kindness and camaraderie of this remarkable group.

Boss cleared his throat, snapping Elena out of her reverie. "For now, it's crucial you stay close to Pup."

Elena hesitated, ready to argue, but he raised his hand to stop her.

"It's the smartest move. Bravo team is heading out on a mission, and the remaining Alpha team members will be joining them. You and Pup are the only ones staying behind."

Elena was taken aback, puzzled by their exclusion. They weren't just handlers. They were agents, too. "But, why aren't we going?"

Boss let out a heavy sigh. "Zee's put you on hold. She might decide to keep her tour going, and if she does, she insists on having the dogs and their handlers by her side every step of the way."

The thought of hitting the road with Pup again was a hard no. No way. No how. They couldn't do it because Aaron would inevitably have them sharing a room, and she knew exactly what would follow.

"Casey can manage it on her own."

Grits beamed with pride, like a father watching his agent and K9 team shine. "I'm sure she and Pup can handle it, but Zee may say differently."

Elena hesitated, unsure why she was debating with her boss. It wasn't his call. It was the client's. "All right." She'd just insist on separate rooms in the contract. Surely the brothers would agree to her privacy.

As the last of the beer and wings vanished, so did the lively crowd, leaving only Boss and Grits behind. When they finally stood up, she found herself in a panic, unsure of how to keep them from leaving her alone with Pup. Any attempt to stall would be transparent, and she risked losing her job over her affair with her subordinate. Daylan. Oh no, she hoped he wouldn't spill the beans about the scandalous scene he'd witnessed at the hotel. She knew she had to have a serious chat with him to keep his lips sealed.

At the door, Boss turned to her. "Do you need anything else?"

Her mind raced with a silent plea: Yes, please don't leave me alone with Pup. But the words refused to escape her lips.

Instead, she shook her head, trying to sound grateful. "No, everyone has been so helpful already." She flashed back to when Cowboy had discreetly cleaned her bathroom mirror, erasing the racial slur Mark had scrawled with her lipstick. Cowboy had assured her to step back, promising to handle it himself. And he had, with the quiet efficiency of a true friend.

"All right, then." Boss nodded to Pup with a firm look. "Keep her safe."

Pup nodded. "I will."

A surge of frustration, along with a scream, bubbled

up inside her. She could handle herself, but at this moment, the thought was overwhelming. Her furniture and mattress were being hauled away to the dump, thanks to Ballpark and his trusty truck. How could she possibly manage? Her friend Jennifer was already juggling three energetic kids and had no spare space. Luis was a friend, but not the kind she could rely on in this situation. She wanted to let out a deep sigh. It was clear she needed to find more dependable friends.

"Good. Good night, you two. See you tomorrow."

With Boss's goodbye, the team leaders departed, leaving Elena standing at the door, her eyes fixed on the spot where their retreating figures would have been if the door hadn't obstructed her view. She couldn't bring herself to turn around and face Pup.

Pup's voice was near. "You know. You'll have to face the music eventually."

She knew it, but the thought made her stomach churn. Reluctantly, she turned to find Pup standing before her, just out of reach. "Oh!" Her skin prickled with goosebumps. "I didn't see you there." She tried to mask her surprise, but she was sure he saw through her.

He gazed down at her, flashing that irresistible smile that sent delicious shivers down her spine. This was going to be a challenge.

"Uh-huh." He casually turned away. "Hungry? Those wings disappeared fast, and I'm ravenous."

She chuckled, trying to hide her amusement, happy he'd lightened the moment. "When aren't you?"

He turned back to her with a nod. "True." As he swung open the refrigerator and freezer, he sighed heavily. "Takeout it is."

"Surely there's something to cook." Her mind was racing with the financial strain of replenishing her apartment and wardrobe. She couldn't afford takeout food. Her family had always been resourceful, crafting delicious, budget-friendly meals in Mexico with their dad, while their mom, who lived in the U.S., was unwell. "What do you have?" She was determined to find a solution.

Pup shrugged. "Not a whole lot of anything. Check for yourself."

With a determined spirit, she rifled through his pantry and freezer: ground meat that needed thawing, potatoes, tomatoes, and frozen mixed vegetables. Her culinary instincts kicked in, and she decided to whip up a simple Mexican dish—Picadillo. However, the spice cabinet was nearly bare, so she slipped to her apartment and grabbed what hadn't been dumped out.

As she prepared the meal, the lively beats of a Latino music station filled the air, providing a comforting distraction from the man in the other room. But now, the moment had arrived to confront him across his modest kitchen table. The universe seemed to conspire against her, as he exuded an undeniable charm.

After warming the rice cups from his cupboard, she proudly presented the meal.

"Wow." He accepted a bowl and took it to the table. After setting it down, he invited her to sit by pulling out a chair with a grace that only heightened her frustration. Why did he have to be so impeccably charming?

I have to remember the age and the boss issues.

Then, she mentally shook her head. They are merely excuses. She reluctantly took her seat, and he hesitated before moving around the table to join her, his presence both captivating and daunting.

He took a bite, chewed, then swallowed. "Your day has been shit, hasn't it?"

She couldn't help but chuckle at his candor. "Yes, it has been."

"While my bed is always open for you to join me, feel free to take the spare room for as long as you need."

Her fork paused mid-air. He really meant for her to sleep in the spare room, not his bed? Okay, he had offered, but this was cause for celebration. Or was it? She pondered, then reconsidered, unsure of her feelings. "Thank you." She quickly stuffed food into her mouth to avoid blurting out something awkward like, "Really? In a separate room? Like that worked the first time?"

"You're welcome." He took another bite and nodded. "This is pretty good."

"Thanks." To steer the conversation away from their romantic entanglement, she shifted the focus to Boss's recent words. "I can't believe Zee put us on hold to jet off with her."

Pup grinned. "Yeah, we get paid to chill until she makes up her mind. It's a pretty sweet gig."

It hadn't occurred to her that they'd be compensated by Zee no matter what, but it was a logical move. As agents, they earned a decent salary, but their real earnings came from bonuses on operations. These bonuses varied, sometimes small, sometimes substantial, depending on the client's budget and the team's involvement. Elena would have to rely on those modest bonuses to piece her life back together.

"Do you reckon the police are getting warmer on the trail of her bomber?" Pup leaned back with a satisfied sigh as he pushed away his empty plate and gave his belly a gentle pat. "Wow, I'm stuffed. That meal was absolutely fantastic."

Elena felt heat rise to her cheeks. "Thanks. I don't know. I can't shake the feeling about that janitor."

Pup nodded. "I didn't catch a glimpse of him, but I can see why he'd stand out."

"I've never seen him before, yet there was something eerily familiar about him."

"What was it?" Pup sipped water and leaned back in his chair. "Tell you what. How about we move this conversation to the living room?"

Elena, ever mindful of any closeness between them, quickly stood up. "I'll handle the dishes." She gathered their plates and rushed into the kitchen, her hands trembling slightly as she set them on the counter.

She started at his unexpected words.

"You forgot the bowls."

His presence was unnervingly close. He reached around her, placing the leftover Picadillo on the counter. "Don't worry. As much as I want to, I'm not going to bite."

How had he managed to sneak up on her like that? She was usually more alert. "I know." She didn't turn to face him.

The air crackled with an electric tension as he leaned in, so close their breaths intertwined. Was he waiting for a sign, a spark? Elena stood rooted, heart pounding, unable to turn. With a heavy sigh, he reluctantly pulled back, leaving the kitchen in a charged silence.

Elena took a deep breath, trying to steady her racing pulse. Just being near him sent it into overdrive. This had to change.

She set about cleaning the plates and loading them into the small dishwasher, then stored the food in a container and tidied the serving dish. As she wiped down the counters and stove, she realized she could no longer avoid the inevitable. With a determined sigh, she set down the dish towel and made her way to the living room, where Pup lounged casually on the couch, a TV remote in hand.

"I could've done those, but you wouldn't move." He finally turned to her, curiosity etched on his face. "Why is that, Elena?"

Her mind raced for a response. What could she possibly say? If she turned, she'd be enveloped in his arms, and that was a temptation she couldn't afford to indulge. "No reason. Just tired. I'm heading to the spare room."

He shrugged casually, his attention returning to the TV. "Mi casa es su casa."

As Elena walked away, she silently vowed to return to her apartment the next day. Sleeping so close to him stirred memories of their unforgettable trip, memories she desperately needed to escape. Yet, as night fell, her dreams were a whirlwind of their past and future possibilities, teasing her with a vision of what could be. When she awoke, drenched in sweat, her heart ablaze, and her core throbbing, she realized that keeping them apart would be far more challenging than she had anticipated.

Chapter Twenty-Three

After a restless night, tossing and turning with thoughts of Elena in the next room, Pup finally dragged himself out of bed, craving a hot shower. But Elena had already claimed it. The temptation to join her was strong, but he held back, trusting that she would figure it out and come to him when the time was right.

What exactly was she supposed to figure out? Even Pup was grappling with his feelings. In his heart, he knew that if it ever came to it, he would leave HIS for Elena, a decision that screamed volumes, yet he wasn't ready to confront it.

Eager to take Casey and Tiki for a stroll, he made his way to the kitchen for a refreshing sip of orange juice. As he reached for the carton, a note caught his eye, and a warm smile spread across his face. She had already taken both dogs for their walk while he was still dreaming of her. Damn. This woman was sinking into his skin.

Meanwhile, Pup found cereal as their only breakfast option. Determined to start the day right, he called a delivery service, ordering breakfast burritos and sandwiches, hoping they'd arrive before Elena was ready to face the day. Then, he'd quickly shower, probably have to jerk off, and get himself together.

They would spend another day with Daylan, but Pup's mind was a whirlwind of thoughts about Elena's tumultuous life. It seemed like she was caught in a storm, and someone—or perhaps a group of someones—was determined to make her life a living hell. What could she have possibly done to provoke such relentless torment?

There had to be a reason. Had she stumbled upon their dirty dealings? That could explain their relentless pursuit. But how far would they go? Blowing up the place she was supposed to call home was beyond anything he could have fathomed.

And then came the shocking series of events—planting drugs, slashing tires, and ransacking her apartment. It was a bewildering sequence, shifting rapidly from one chaos to another. Disjointed and intense, it left a strong impression on Elena, stirring a mix of fear and confusion.

The front buzzer interrupted his musings. Pressing the intercom, Pup said, "Yes?"

"Delivery for Kevin Richards."

"Come on in." He buzzed the door, allowing the delivery woman to enter. As he opened his door, he greeted her warmly. "Thank you." He accepted the bag of food and two cups of coffee. Though he wasn't a coffee drinker, he knew Elena loved it and wanted her to have plenty.

As he savored a bite of his burrito, Elena emerged from the bathroom, exuding an undeniable badass vibe in her tight HIS T-shirt and all-black ensemble. She looked like a mercenary, and it made his dick twitch for her. He wanted to reach out and pull her into him and fuck her senseless. But instead—

She broke into his thoughts as she cautiously made her way over. "Oh, food. I'll pay you back." She reached into the bag he offered and snatched a sandwich, then let out a delighted squeal at the sight of the coffee. "For me?"

Pup chuckled at her enthusiasm. "Yes. And no, you won't pay me back. I had to eat."

She sipped her java. "But you didn't have to get it for me."

Frustrated, he set down his half-eaten burrito and placed his hands on his hips. "When are you going to learn that we're a family, and family doesn't have to 'pay' family back in any manner?"

Elena set her coffee down softly on the table and swallowed hard, the lump in her throat visible to him. "It's just still…new to me. That's all." Her voice was barely above a whisper.

He raised an eyebrow, a hint of challenge in his gaze. "Well, learn quicker." With that, he reached for his breakfast, the morning light casting a warm glow on his movements. As he made his way to his bedroom, he grabbed his clothes, taking another bite. By the time he reached the bathroom, his breakfast was already a memory.

The cold water hit him like a wake-up call, and as he stood there, thoughts of Elena in her outfit danced through his mind. The intensity of the moment was overwhelming, and when he finally reached his peak, it took every ounce of his willpower not to let her name escape his lips.

With a sense of calm returning, Pup and Elena efficiently loaded the dogs into his truck. Elena had a rental car waiting for them later, a decision that didn't sit well with Pup, but he respected her need for space. The drive was mostly silent, punctuated by Elena's reminders about the rental and Pup's grumbling in response.

Upon arriving at HIS headquarters, they were greeted by Daylan and Buddy. "Thought I'd save you the walk to the kennels." Daylan smiled charmingly at Elena and nodded to Pup.

Pup's mood soured instantly. If Daylan dared to flirt with Elena, he was ready to pounce, regardless of the agent's height. Pup's fighting skills were nothing to scoff at.

With the dogs trotting beside them, they made their way to the obstacle course for agility practice. Casey had already mastered the course, but Pup noticed Elena's dissatisfaction with Buddy's performance, so he decided to follow along.

Devon intercepted them. "You're needed at HQ. Zee has decided to continue her tour."

Daylan flashed a grin. "See you guys around." He turned to leave.

As Pup prepared to join the group, Devon stopped him. "You're not needed, Pup."

Pup froze. "What?"

Devon shrugged. "You can come, but they only want Elena and Tiki."

Pup's hopes of spending some quality time with Elena faded, leaving him with a bittersweet realization.

****

Elena's head throbbed as she sat through the briefing, which was a rehash of the basics from the first one, but now with an added twist that they only wanted her and her dog alone. At least the private jet was on its way to whisk them away.

"Elena, can I have a word with you in private?" Jesse asked once the group had scattered.

"I'll take Tiki out with us." Pup gave her a knowing grin.

Though she didn't want to depend on him, Tiki desperately needed a bathroom break, and she couldn't manage it now. "Thanks."

Once they were alone, Jesse turned to her. "Emily is taking you shopping on the company credit card."

She started to protest, but he quickly raised his hand. "You can pay it back whenever you can. You need clothes for this tour, and we look out for our own."

He probably knew she'd have to sell a CD to access her savings. They seemed to know everything else.

Accepting her fate, she forced a smile. "Thank you."

"Don't worry about it. The teams are all set to bring the promised items to your apartment, so I think it's best to wrap up your day and let them get started."

Overwhelmed, she fought the tears wanting to burst forward. "It's just so much." She took a deep breath. "Thank you, Jesse. You won't regret giving us a chance."

His golden-brown eyes twinkled with determination. "We don't. Now, let's talk about your other issue."

She tensed, uncertain of his stance on her lawsuit.

"This will keep you safe while we assist the police in

their investigation. The teams will be gone, but my brothers, our wives, and I are fully committed to handling this."

She blinked against the pressure building, denying the tears the dignity of falling. "Do you know?" She had trusted Boss to inform those he deemed necessary, and she assumed Jesse was among them.

"I know. And I support you completely. If you ever feel harassed on my teams, come straight to me because I won't stand for it."

She trusted him and felt confident in her decision. But then, a wave of guilt washed over her as she recalled tossing aside their rules for a brief moment of passion. "Jesse." She felt compelled to confess. She couldn't let the secret linger. While she didn't want anyone else to know, she needed him to be aware.

He raised an eyebrow. "Yes?"

Taking a deep breath, she glanced around the room, ensuring no one was listening. They were completely alone. Even Devon had abandoned his beloved keyboard. "I—" She closed her eyes tightly before opening them again. "—I broke a rule."

Jesse tilted his head, encouraging her to continue. "Go on."

"I, uh, slept with a subordinate."

To her surprise, he didn't react with shock. Instead, he simply smiled.

"Did you hear me?"

Jesse nodded, his expression turning serious. "Daylan already shared his suspicions."

Damn Daylan. That big mouth. She had felt that she

couldn't rely on him when it mattered most.

"Elena, as long as it doesn't impact your work relationship and the subordinate doesn't feel pressured, then it's fine." He flashed a reassuring smile. "Should I have a chat with Pup about whether you're coercing him into something?"

"No. I'd prefer he didn't know I confided in you."

Jesse gestured for her to take a seat at the briefing table, joining her. "Elena, I need to speak with Pup. I trust you, but we must ensure nothing like what happened to you—"

His hand gently stopped her from protesting.

"I know you weren't coerced. Wouldn't you want the same if the roles were reversed?"

She wanted to shake her head in denial, as it would be embarrassing, but he was right. It also protected the company.

Worry gnawed at her gut like a relentless beast. "So, I'm not fired?" Please say I'm not fired. Please.

"Elena." His tone turned serious. "Do you want to continue a relationship with Pup, or was it just a onetime thing?"

She hesitated, the words "onetime thing" on her lips, but she knew she was lying. She hadn't wanted a relationship after leaving her last one, yet the thought of a sexually satisfying connection was tempting.

"I really don't know." Her honesty was surprising even to herself.

"Well, figure it out. If it impacts HIS, then it stops, no matter how you feel about it."

"Yes, sir." Her resolve was strengthening. She loved

her job too much to let anything jeopardize it. Maybe this trip alone was a good idea. As much as she craved to be in Pup's bed, it was wiser to wait until she had everything sorted out.

Devon burst into the room. "Jesse, you need to step outside right now!"

Jesse jumped up. "What's happening?"

Devon's eyes widened. "Pup just delivered a knockout punch to Daylan."

Chapter Twenty-Four

Pain surged through Pup's fist, but his fury was so intense that it barely registered. The asshole had spread his suspicions that Pup had been with Elena. If Elena lost her job because of this, Pup vowed to unleash more than just a punch on the man.

Dammit. He fervently hoped Daylan had only confided in Jesse, as he had said, and not spilled the beans to the entire team. He couldn't bear the thought of Elena's reputation being marred. But if Daylan had indeed damaged it, Pup was at a loss for how to mend the situation.

He looked down at Daylan. "At least a dog is loyal."

Jesse stormed out of the building, with Elena and Devon hot on his trail.

"What the hell happened here?" Jesse knelt beside the unconscious Daylan to check his pulse, as if Pup had possibly killed him.

"You know what the hell happened." Pup's retort was firmer than he should have been to his boss, but his gaze was fixed on Elena, who was visibly shocked by the sight of him nursing his bruised knuckles.

Jesse rose to his feet. "This is not how we handle disputes, Pup. Inside. Now." With that sharp demand, Jesse turned and marched back to HQ, disappearing inside.

Elena approached him, concern etched on her face. "Are you all right?" She gently reached out. He showed her his battered knuckles, a silent testament to the punch he'd landed.

"He told." Pup hoped she would piece together the puzzle.

Understanding dawned on her face, and she nodded solemnly. "I know. You should get inside before he returns."

"Please, take care of Casey for me."

"Of course."

As Daylan let out a groan, Pup determinedly made his way to HQ, navigating through the security protocols with resolve. Inside, Jesse stood at the briefing table, arms crossed, exuding an aura of anger.

Pup's heart pounded as he nearly shouted his apologies to his boss, the formidable figure who could end his career with a single word. He clung to the hope that it wouldn't come to that.

Jesse, with a slightly calmer demeanor, gestured to the chairs. "Have a seat, Pup."

Pup sank into the chair, bracing himself for the inevitable ass-chewing. As he squirmed uncomfortably, Pup repeated his apologies, hoping to soften the blow to a mere lecture.

Jesse leaned forward, his voice steady. "We can't

have this type of behavior, Pup. What brought it on?"

Pup narrowed his eyes, his frustration evident. "You know what he did."

Jesse nodded, acknowledging the situation. "I do. But that doesn't give you the right to resort to violence." Jesse leaned back in his chair with a confident air, arms crossed. "What are we going to do about this?"

Pup's mind went blank, but he knew he couldn't dodge the consequences of his actions. "I don't know."

"You realize Daylan could sue us, right?"

Pup's body tensed. "He wouldn't." It was incredulous at the thought of someone suing a company trained for violence with violence. It was almost surreal.

"He could. I doubt he will, but that doesn't change the fact that you hit him. What if you caused serious harm? You did knock him out, after all."

Despite the temptation to grin at the memory of knocking the asshole out with one punch, Pup bit his lip, staying silent instead of grumbling that he didn't do serious harm.

"Pup, consider this a disciplinary warning."

Jesse's words hit Pup like a punch to the gut. He sat up, brows arched, staring at his boss. "What?" He'd never faced such a warning before. But then, a glimmer of hope ignited. They weren't going to fire him.

"You heard me. We can't have this."

"I promise it won't happen again."

"It better not. Now, let's shift gears. I've got some questions for you."

Uh-oh. What had he done this time? Pup's mind raced, replaying every word and action from recent days, but nothing came to mind.

"As you know, I'm aware of your relationship with Elena."

Pup hesitated a response, reluctant to label it a relationship just yet.

"I need to know if you entered it willingly?"

Pup's eyes widened in shock, leaning forward in disbelief. "Do you mean did she force me?"

Jesse nodded. "Yes."

He leaned back, shaking his head. "Not in the least." Pup wondered if Boss and Sugar had faced similar challenges before she left HIS. It was a fleeting thought, but it slid by.

"I need to know, immediately, if you ever feel coerced."

Pup raised his hand, a daring gesture that silenced his boss. "I like her. I didn't at first, but I do now. I instigated it all and probably will again."

"Pup."

"But only if she's willing."

Jesse nodded, acknowledging the delicate balance. "Okay. Just be careful. You two are walking a fine line." With those words, Jesse abruptly rose, bringing the conversation to a halt.

As Devon and Elena made their entrance, Jesse beckoned Elena over. "I need a quick word about the op."

Pup felt no need to concern himself and instead approached Devon. "What's happening, Devon?" His curiosity was piqued by Devon's expression.

Devon flashed a mischievous grin. "When you do it, you do it big."

Pup's face lit up with a wide smile, echoing Devon's enthusiasm. "Yep."

After Jesse's conversation with Elena, they slipped away from HIS, heading to her apartment just in time for the other agents' arrival. She had already canceled the rental, knowing she'd be off by morning, which meant more precious time alone for them on the drive to the airport. The air in the cab of his truck was thick with unspoken words, and Pup was at a loss for how to ease the tension.

As they neared halfway home, Elena broke the silence. "I can't believe you hit him."

Pup shot her a quick glance before refocusing on the road. "I did. He deserved it."

"He did. I'm glad you hit him."

Her words caught him off guard. "Really?" He turned to her again, this time holding her gaze longer, until the truck's lane alert beeped, reminding him he'd veered off course. He quickly corrected the vehicle, his mind still racing with her unexpected approval.

"I don't condone violence. Well, except when necessary. But he'd earned it."

Pup nodded. "Yep."

Silence enveloped them once more, and Pup felt it was time to lay his heart on the line. "What are we going to do?"

Elena hesitated, her gaze fixed ahead. "About what?"

"About us."

If she turned to him, he could read the emotions in her eyes. But each time he glanced over, she remained facing forward.

"There is no us. That was a mistake." Her words cut through the air.

Pup's heart skipped a beat as he slammed on the brakes, skillfully maneuvering the truck to the side of the road. He shifted into Park and turned to face her, determination burning in his eyes. "Let's try that again."

She finally turned, her expression a mix of pain and something else—something he couldn't quite place. But he knew she felt it too. The air between them always buzzed with an undeniable energy, a connection that wasn't just his imagination. And by all that was holy, their time together had not been a mistake.

"Pup—"

He instinctively knew to stop her before she could finish. He'd used the "It's not you. It's me" line too many times to let it slide.

"No. We have something undeniable, Elena. Our time together wasn't a mistake. If Daylan hadn't interrupted, we would've spent the entire night discovering each other's bodies and making love."

As she prepared to respond, Pup raised his hand to silence her.

"And you can't deny it, can you? That certain spark between us."

Elena bit her lip, and he thought he saw tears glistening in her eyes, but maybe he was imagining things, because she quickly regained her composure. "So, we have chemistry? That doesn't mean we have to act on it. I'm your boss, Pup. I'm much older than you. You don't even like me. We have nothing but a few sparks. Let it go."

Pup was determined not to back down but to face the

unexpected roadblocks she was setting up.

Just then, a truck laden with furniture screeched to a halt in front of him, reversing ominously closer.

"Great." Why did the men have to stop and check on him? Sure, they might have been stranded, but still….

"Is that my new furniture?" Her eyes were fixed on the truck.

"Don't change the subject." His retort was sharper than intended. This was overwhelming.

"There's nothing more to discuss." She waved to Ballpark, who had stepped out of the truck.

Pup let it slide for now, but he wasn't ready to give up on her. An instinct told him to fight for her, to cling to her even when they clashed. That's just how couples are. And there it was—he wanted them to be a couple. The realization hit him like a bolt of lightning and tossed him off-balance.

As he turned to Ballpark, he defiantly flipped him the bird, prompting the agent to chuckle and retreat to his truck, shaking his head.

"Why did you do that? He was just checking on us."

"Because these men are a bunch of nosy-bodies."

He straightened up, put the truck in gear, and navigated back onto the highway. He was determined to unravel the mystery of why he wanted to be with someone who clearly didn't share the same desire. And with her out of pocket for the unforeseeable future, he, unfortunately, had plenty of time to figure it out.

Chapter Twenty-Five

After the furniture delivery, Emily arrived right on time, whisking Elena away for a shopping spree. As they strolled through the bustling department stores on Townsend, Elena couldn't help but reminisce about her first truce with Pup and their memorable shopping adventure.

This time, however, the experience was blissfully free of the usual snooty salespeople. Emily's keen eye for a bargain ensured they found the perfect outfits for Elena, all within an amount she felt she could comfortably repay. With her new wardrobe and sturdy luggage—a necessary upgrade after her soft-sided one met a sorry fate—Elena set to packing once more.

To her relief, her SUV had been returned while she'd been shopping, sparing her the need to hitch a ride with Pup to the airport. Lost in thought about whether she was thrilled or not, she initially missed the noise.

When her phone buzzed with a call from a friend, she hesitated for a moment, tempted to let it go. But then, she thought, why not take a break from the usual chatter about Zee, HIS, and her complicated relationship with

Pup?

Elena sank onto the well-worn, pale green and white-striped couch that the agents had generously donated. "Hi, Jennifer."

"Where have you been? I tried to stop by today, but you weren't home."

Elena, usually a private person, had kept her recent experiences to herself. But today, something changed. The words spilled out like a torrent, starting with the explosion that had shattered her world.

Jennifer had known Elena was leaving Mark, but that was the last time they had truly connected. Initially, Elena was too shaken by the explosion to share her story.

Now, Jennifer listened intently, unable to interrupt as Elena recounted the explosion, the drugs, the tires, and the chaos of her trashed apartment.

Jennifer took a deep breath, her eyes wide with disbelief. "You mean he trashed the couch I gave you?"

Elena chuckled softly, appreciating her friend's attempt to lighten the mood. "Yes, he did. The chairs, too."

"Bastard." Jennifer's playful tone gave way to genuine anger. "I'd like to kick Mark's ass myself. What are you going to do now? Joking aside, this sounds serious, Elena."

Elena knew it was serious, but with her departure looming indefinitely, her options were limited. She shrugged, feeling a mix of frustration and helplessness. "I don't know. HIS said they'd look into it for me, so I have to trust them."

"But think, you get to jet-set with Zee Alvarez. How

cool is that?"

Elena wasn't as enthusiastic as Jennifer, but she forced a smile and nodded. "It is cool." Though her heart wasn't in it now that Pup wouldn't be traveling with her. It set off her "what the hell am I going to do?" internal conversation.

Just then, a knock echoed through the room. Her heart lurched, expecting Pup to be there to "talk" again. She sighed heavily. "Listen, I have to finish packing."

"Give me a ring while you're on the road. It sounds like you could use a friend."

As they were about to hang up, her friend added, "Oh, by the way, how did things go with that other handler? The one who was eyeing your spot?"

Elena couldn't suppress a laugh. "That's a whole other tale I'll save for later."

"Oh, I'm holding you to that." Her friend chuckled.

After ending the call, Elena stood up, determined to push Pup aside. It was a tough spot. She wanted him. She couldn't deny it. But not at the cost of her job or her peace of mind. Without checking who was there, she opened the door, and her breath hitched, her heart skipping a beat. She couldn't believe her eyes. "Mark."

She peered down the hallway, her eyes narrowing at the unexpected intruder. "How the hell did you get in here?" Her mind raced to the careless neighbor who must've left the brick wedged open again. She'd have a stern chat with them later.

Her gaze shifted to Mark, and she was taken aback by his unkempt state. His hair was a wild mess, and a faint beard shadowed his face. It was a stark contrast to the impeccably groomed man she once knew.

Despite his appearance, her feelings were clear. "What do you want?"

"We need to talk, Elena."

She stood firm, her anger barely contained. "No, we don't. You need to leave."

"It's important." He attempted to push past her into her apartment.

Elena blocked his path, her voice steady. "Leave. Don't you think you've done enough damage?"

He exhaled a heavy sigh, appearing a decade older than his years. "I know what I've done, but you have to listen."

She hesitated, her hand hovering over the doorknob, when the memory of his actions flashed through her mind. "No. Leave." With a decisive slam, she shut the door in his face, a satisfying sense of empowerment washing over her. He didn't knock again, but she could feel his presence lingering outside, waiting. She was determined to outlast him. After a tense few minutes, she heard his heavy footsteps retreating down the hall. Taking a moment to gather her courage, she cautiously peeked down the empty corridor and then headed to the front door, ensuring it was securely locked. Thankfully, there was no brick.

Pup startled her. "What are you doing?"

"Oh, just checking for the brick." She turned to face him, and her heart skipped a beat.

There he stood, clad in his black cargo pants, shirtless.

"I—Uh. I have to pack." She tried to move past his

apartment.

"Elena, why not step inside for a moment?"

Because I might lose myself in you, looking like that, and drive us both wild. "I really have to pack."

"Just one drink." He retreated into his apartment, leaving the door ajar for her decision.

Dammit. She truly needed to pack, but the thought of one more night with Pup sent her heart racing. Then, in a moment of impulsivity that she might later regret, she followed him inside and closed the door behind them.

As she stepped inside, hesitation gripped her at the threshold, making her question her every move. She could turn back and avoid the inevitable, knowing that staying would lead to something significant. Yet, she was weary of always choosing the right path. She craved the freedom to follow her heart. And her heart yearned for Pup with an intensity she couldn't ignore.

"Here." He opened a bottle of beer and handed it to her, their bottles clinking in silent understanding.

"Thanks." Before Elena could sip, Pup took the bottle from her hand, placing both on the table by the door.

"Fuck it." His hand found its way to the back of her neck, pulling her close. "I want you in my bed, Elena."

Her burning desire matched his. "Then kiss me."

When their lips collided, heat flared, drawing her into the intoxicating blend of his taste and the lingering hint of beer. The kiss deepened—slow at first, then hungry. She wrapped her arms around his neck, feeling the electric charge as he pressed his firmness against her.

He broke the kiss. "If you want to turn back, now's

the time. Because I'm not letting you go tonight."

She caught the word "tonight" and not "forever," and it was perfect. She wasn't ready for forever either. Tonight was enough. It had to be. After all, she was leaving in the morning, possibly for a long time. Who knew when they'd have another chance like this?

She seized the moment. "I'm not going anywhere."

He gently took her arms from around his neck, his touch electric. "Come." He led her with a soft pull toward the bedroom—the very room she had longed for the night before, only to resist and emerge victorious. Yet, the victory had left her with an unfulfilled longing, a hollow prize indeed.

"You've got too many clothes on." His fingers brushed against her T-shirt.

She nodded, lifting her arms as he deftly slipped the shirt over her head, her braid cascading down her shoulder.

"You have such beautiful hair. I want it down."

Not one to argue over something so trivial, she reached for the hair tie.

"No, let me." He carefully removed the tie and slowly unraveled her braid, each touch igniting a spark within her.

As her hair cascaded over her shoulders, he gently spread it out, drawing some strands across her chest. A playful smile danced on his lips as he caressed her hair. "I've never been with a woman whose hair reaches their butt."

She responded by reaching for his chest. "And I've never been with a man who shaved his chest."

Their eyes met, and the world seemed to pause.

"I believe you owe me some exploration time." His voice was a sultry whisper.

Heat surged through her at the thought of his lips exploring every inch of her body. She'd never been daring, but something grabbed hold of her will and roused it. "Well, let's get to it."

He chuckled softly, his fingers skillfully unclasping her bra with practiced ease. "These are perfect." His hands gently cradled her breasts, his thumbs teasing the sensitive peaks, sending shivers down her spine.

A soft moan escaped her, the pleasure of his touch intoxicating, yet it only fueled her desire for more. With a determined glint in her eye, she reached for his pants, deftly unbuttoning them before sliding them down his legs.

"Boots." He momentarily released her to sit on the edge of the bed.

Elena, having already shed her shoes at her apartment, seized the moment. As he untied his boots, she moved with a sense of urgency, removing the rest of her clothing, each piece falling away as if drawn by an invisible force.

He rose and peeled off his pants and underwear. She couldn't help but be captivated by his striking appearance and impressive length. A thrill coursed through her at the thought of his cock inside her.

"You. Get on the bed and let me have my way with you."

She giggled, slipping past him with a playful leap onto the bed, where she lay down, arms wide open, and grinned. "I'm all yours."

With a low growl, he joined her on the bed. "That's what I want."

Her heart paused. Did he truly mean what he said, or was it just playful banter during foreplay? Perhaps he hadn't caught the nuance in her words. She hadn't intended them to mean more than the moment, but did his words carry a deeper significance like hers?

"Where'd you go?" His warm breath sent a shiver down her spine as it tickled her ear.

She brought herself back to the present. "I'm right here."

After gently nibbling on her ear, he let a trail of scorching kisses cascade down her chest, each one igniting its own spark of desire. He paused and tenderly sucked on her firm nipple, sending waves of heat coursing through her body, eliciting a soft moan of pure pleasure.

"I'll return to these." His voice held a promise as he ventured further down her stomach. "I have a target in mind."

The thought of his destination sent her nearly soaring off the bed, anticipation dancing at her core as he playfully teased her belly button.

Chapter Twenty-Six

"Your skin is like silk." His voice was a gentle caress as he journeyed deeper. "So irresistibly inviting."

She managed a soft "thanks," barely audible over the crescendo of her heartbeat. His touch was a dance of fire and delight, igniting every nerve.

"At last." His breath was a warm promise against her core. "I've been waiting to savor you."

As his tongue touched her for the first time, she arched off the bed, the sensation a thrilling blaze.

His warm tongue danced over her core, sending shivers of delight through her body as she writhed beneath his tender ministrations. When he gently slipped a finger inside, a surge of pleasure nearly propelled her off the bed.

He paused, lifting his head with a satisfied smile, his finger still moving rhythmically. "You taste so perfect." His voice was a soft caress.

She glanced down at him, a playful smile playing on her lips. Usually, the thought of a man going down on her made her blush, but with Pup? It was a different story. He could do this forever, as far as she was concerned. His touch was nothing short of enchanting.

As he watched her, he gently slid a second finger inside her, his voice a soft murmur of admiration. "My. My. You're more than ready for me."

Her body responded eagerly, the wet heat between her legs a testament to her desire. She was teetering on the edge of climax, her breath coming in short, urgent pants. "I want to come with you inside me." With her voice barely audible, she wasn't sure he heard her.

He chuckled softly, removing his fingers with a teasing smile. "You don't have to ask me twice." With a playful roll, he reached for a condom from the drawer in his bedside table.

"Handy." A hint of jealousy tinged with curiosity about who might have used that stash before.

"Jealous? I've never brought a woman home. These, I put here for us."

Her heart swelled with emotion, and a realization washed over her like a gentle wave. I'm in love with him.

An unexpected jolt surged through her heart, leaving her breathless. How could she be falling for a man so much younger? Sure, he was incredible in bed, but surely there was more to it. Wasn't there?

Perhaps her heart had already decided, and she needed to trust it wasn't just a fleeting passion. All she had to do was resist the urge to shout it out during the heat of the moment or in the blissful aftermath, like so many others did.

With the condom securely in place, he lay back and pulled her onto him. "Kiss me." His smile was so irresistible that it would've brought her to her knees had she been standing.

As if under a spell, she leaned in, capturing his lips and taking charge of a kiss that sent electric waves coursing through her already racing heart.

As Elena's lips danced over his, his hands traced soothing paths down her back, teasing the hair that brushed against her lower back. Suddenly, he gripped her ass, pulling her closer against his undeniable erection.

Pup broke the kiss. "I need to be inside you."

Though she was known for arguing with him, this wasn't the time. Instead, she took charge, straddling him, and guided him to her core. With a slow, deliberate descent, she surrendered to the overwhelming sensation of his fullness and the electrifying pleasure that surged through her.

She paused, savoring the sensation of him pulsing within her, amplifying her already exhilarating excitement. "You feel incredible inside me." She began to move with deliberate grace.

Her eyes met Pup's, who watched with an intensity that mirrored her own, as he effortlessly slid in and out of her.

How could she have fallen for this man so swiftly? Surely, it was just a passing emotion. Yet, deep down, she knew it was something far more profound—the genuine article.

As she moved, he pulled her closer, rolling them over so he was on top. She wrapped her legs around his waist, and he adjusted his position, entering her deeply and sending a jolt through her system.

"You're amazing. I want you to come."

She was on the brink, her desire burning intensely. As their bodies glistened with sweat and their breaths quickened, she felt the exhilarating ascent. "Oh, Kevin, I'm so close." She moaned her pleasure.

With a subtle shift, he sent her spiraling into a breathtaking climax, shattering into a thousand delicate fragments floating through the sky.

Exhausted and content, she barely noticed him pulsing inside her before he reached his peak.

With a heavy sigh, he collapsed beside her, his breath ragged. "Wow."

"Wow."

"I need a minute."

She agreed. Their intense climax left her breathless.

"I need to get rid of this condom. I'll be right back." He rose and left.

As she watched him go, she pondered what it was about this young man that had captured her heart so completely.

When he returned, he enveloped her in a warm embrace, holding her close. "Are you certain you don't need a ride to the airport in the morning?"

She longed to linger and spend more time with him, but her SUV had been returned, giving her the freedom to travel. She hoped it wouldn't fall victim to slashed tires and would be waiting for her upon her return, though she had no clue when that might be.

The thought of being apart from him for an uncertain period tugged at her heartstrings. Would he remember her during her absence? Would he find someone else?

She pushed those unsettling thoughts aside.

"Elena?"

Startled back to reality, she shook her head. "No, I'm fine."

"All right. Just wake me before you leave."

She knew she wouldn't, but she promised anyway.

As they dozed off, Elena wondered where this relationship would go now that she knew her heart. Would he find the same love for her? She hoped so because she didn't think she could handle working with him and not having him in her life.

****

Elena awoke unexpectedly, her heart fluttering as she gazed at Pup, who lay peacefully on his back, emitting a charming little snore. The moment was irresistibly endearing, and she felt a playful urge to pounce on him, but duty called. She knew she had to leave.

Determined to avoid a dramatic farewell, Elena tiptoed out of bed, carefully gathering her pants and underwear. Her T-shirt was still in the living room, a reminder of the night before. There, she dressed quietly, casting one final, wistful glance at the bedroom where she had discovered her love for Pup. With a heavy heart, she slipped out of his apartment and headed back to her own.

Once inside, Elena quickly showered, her mind racing with thoughts of the impending departure. She had to pack swiftly because her flight was scheduled for the early hours. Even private jets adhered to such demanding schedules.

With a sense of excitement, she swiftly packed her

new clothes into her suitcase, then took Tiki outside for one last night adventure. Back inside, she tucked the K9 into her cozy dog bed before Elena herself settled into bed for a brief nap, setting her alarm for the early hours of three a.m. The flight was scheduled for four, and the journey to the airport would take some time.

It felt like just a moment had passed when the alarm jolted her awake. Tiki was already by her side, her tail wagging eagerly for morning cuddles.

"Come on, girl." Elena patted the bed. Tiki leaped up with grace, settling on Elena's chest. "Good grief, you're getting heavy."

Tiki playfully nudged Elena's chin with her nose.

Elena chuckled. "Okay."

She knew a few extra minutes of petting and chatting with Tiki wouldn't delay her, so she savored the moment, her mind drifting back to the earlier hours spent with Pup.

"You know, girl."

The dog playfully licked her chin.

"We've fallen for that man, and it could be a recipe for disaster."

What if Pup decided he was done now that they'd shared a few intimate moments? Could he be one of those fleeting types? She barely knew him, yet here she was, convinced she was in love. Her heart had a mind of its own, and she'd never felt this way about Mark or any other long-term partner.

So why did it have to choose someone so utterly unsuitable? What would Jesse think if they became a couple? How would she handle work if they didn't? With time slipping away, she realized she could mull over these thoughts on the flight.

She quickly dressed in something nice to avoid any awkwardness with Aaron, then braided her hair, recalling how Pup had gently loosened it. "Get a grip!" She needed to focus on today, not last night.

With a sense of anticipation, she instructed Tiki to wait while she prepared for her departure, loading her luggage into the SUV. The journey ahead was uncertain, and she needed more than just her cozy cargo pants and T-shirt, so two suitcases were in order. As she carried them outside, she silently passed Pup's apartment, hoping not to wake him.

At her SUV, she unlocked the trunk with a simple press of the keyfob and began loading her bags, wishing Pup could join her on this trip. She couldn't fathom why Zee had changed her mind from wanting both of them to now only her, but it was a disappointment.

Absorbed in her thoughts, she overlooked the danger until a stun gun jolted her back to reality.

Dammit. Pain surged through her as her muscles locked up. She caught a whiff of her attacker—Mark.

As the shock waves continued, darkness began to encroach on her vision, and she realized she was in grave trouble. But she vowed to outsmart Mark when the opportunity arose.

As consciousness slipped away, she heard him say, "I'm sorry."

His apology meant nothing to her. He would regret it when she was no longer helpless. Then, darkness enveloped her, and she collapsed.

Chapter Twenty-Seven

Pup jolted awake, his heart racing as he rolled over to find Elena missing. A groan escaped him as he glanced at the clock—nearly five a.m. How could he have slept so deeply? Memories of their passionate moments flooded back. He had hoped to see her off this morning, but it seemed she had chosen to slip away silently.

Determined, he resolved to win her when she returned. She would be his, in every sense, for he was utterly in love with her.

Without Elena's morning training, he had the luxury of a later start at HQ, not needing to arrive until eight a.m. The extra hour of sleep beckoned, but his mind was a whirlwind of memories—her soft skin, her enchanting body, and those mesmerizing eyes. Accepting that sleep was elusive, he rose from bed and headed to the shower. This time, he was content, with no urgent needs to attend to. Sure, he could indulge in another round, but patience was an option, too.

As the warm water cascaded over him, he lathered his chest and pondered his day ahead with all the teams out, except for the mysterious Charlie team. Their whereabouts were a mystery. He hoped he wouldn't be stuck with the asshole Daylan.

The memory of Daylan's betrayal had him scrubbing with fervor. Realizing he was overdoing it, he rinsed off and stepped out of the shower, wrapping himself in a towel. With no one around, he confidently marched naked back to his bedroom to get dressed.

Dressed in his work attire, he grabbed Casey's leash with a smile. "Time for you to take care of business." Her tail wagged excitedly as she dashed toward the door.

With a chuckle, he secured her leash and picked up a bag to collect her waste along the way. But as he opened the door, something unexpected happened. Instead of heading to the front door, Casey tugged down the hallway.

It had been ages since she had last pulled like this, not since her unruly puppy days.

"Casey, come on." A sense of unease crept in. He couldn't shake the feeling that something was off. Suddenly, Casey barked, and Tiki responded in kind.

Instinctively, Pup sprinted towards Elena's apartment, fear coursing through his veins.

He pounded on the door, his heart pounding in his chest. "Elena!" His voice echoed in the silence. He jiggled the doorknob—unlocked. A chill of dread slid up his spine. She was supposed to be at the airport by now. Oversleeping was out of the question. Something was wrong.

Stepping inside, Tiki greeted him with a whine. He gave the dog a quick pat before darting through the two-bedroom apartment, scanning every corner. Elena was nowhere to be found. She wouldn't abandon Tiki. The dog was the whole reason for the trip with Zee.

"Bleib," he commanded both dogs, then sprinted out of the apartment, his mind racing.

In the parking lot, his worst fears were confirmed. Her SUV was there. He circled it, his eyes catching every detail, every clue. Something had happened to Elena. He fumbled for his phone, his hands trembling as he dialed HQ.

When a sleepy Devon answered, he cut him off without a second thought. "Elena's been taken." He was sure of it, and he was determined to find her.

In his gut, he felt a deep conviction that the SWAT team was behind her disappearance. They had been the ones targeting her from the start. Though the reasons remained a mystery, he was determined to uncover the truth, and those responsible would face the consequences if they dared to harm her.

"Does she have her phone?"

Devon's computer prowess was legendary, and his ability to track her location through her phone was both awe-inspiring and terrifying. Recalling her purse, just inside the front door of her apartment, a wave of dread washed over him. "I don't know." His heart plummeted to his stomach.

"It's okay. We're on our way. Call the police."

The thought of calling the authorities knotted his gut. It would alert SWAT to their awareness of her absence, potentially forcing them to act prematurely. "Are you sure?"

A soft, husky voice echoed in the background—Rylee, Devon's wife. "I wouldn't. Not yet, anyhow."

Pup nodded, his eyes scanning the parking lot for any anomalies. Apart from Elena's SUV still parked there, everything seemed normal. The small lot was filled with familiar vehicles belonging to tenants.

"Stand by on that call. Just wait for us." With that, Devon ended the call, leaving the tension hanging in the air.

Under the dim glow of streetlights, the parking lot stretched out ominously, and he knew he was powerless until dawn. The thought of her out there, in danger, twisted his heart into knots. He retreated inside, where the two loyal dogs sat patiently, having obeyed his "stay" command. With a deep breath, he released them, and a spark of hope ignited in his mind.

"Tiki, my girl." A smile tugged at his lips. "How good are you at tracking?"

As if sensing his urgency, Tiki barked in response.

Pup's spirits lifted. Maybe, just maybe, Tiki could lead them to her. But then reality hit him like a cold wave. If she had been taken in a vehicle, which seemed all too probable, Tiki's tracking skills would be useless. The dog wasn't magical, after all.

Frustration boiled over, and he clenched his fist, resisting the urge to punch the wall. How dare they take his woman?

The anticipation of the men's arrival stretched endlessly, each second feeling like an eternity. He knew the brothers resided near HQ, just a forty-minute drive away, but that seemed like an insurmountable distance.

Suddenly, the front door buzzed, breaking the silence. It had to be Boss. He lived the closest.

Without hesitation, he pressed the door release button, swung the door open, and shouted down the hallway. "I'm in Elena's apartment."

Boss and his wife, Sugar—a former SWAT and HIS team member—quickly approached. They immediately noticed the anguish in his eyes, prompting Sugar to hug him. "Oh, Kevin, we'll find her."

His gut twisted. They had to find her—now. The SWAT team had already attempted to eliminate her. If they reached her first, would they finish it clean or make her suffer? He shut his eyes, refusing to entertain those dark thoughts.

Sugar released him.

Boss caught his eye. "What do you know?" They stepped into Elena's apartment. The dogs greeted them enthusiastically, and both he and Sugar took a moment to pet them.

"Nothing. She was supposed to leave early for the airport."

Boss scanned the room, then turned back to Pup. "I thought you were taking her."

Pup shrugged, a mix of frustration and helplessness in his expression. "They delivered her SUV back, and she wanted to drive."

He had dreaded her decision the night before. Had it even been night? It felt like just hours since they had been wrapped in each other's arms.

"I told you to stick close to her." Boss jabbed his finger accusingly at him. Pup had stayed close, but Boss didn't need to know just how close.

"She's a grown woman and a HIS agent. What am I supposed to do? Carry her over my shoulder like a caveman and keep her wrapped in bubble wrap?"

Sugar gently placed a hand on Boss's back, prompting him to take a deep breath and exhale slowly. "I'm sorry."

"Look, I didn't like it either. I planned to wake up and see her off, but I overslept." He had intended to escort her out of his apartment after their night together, but that hadn't happened.

"Where do you think she was taken?" Boss's voice was tinged with urgency.

Pup pondered for a moment. "Outside. If it had been in the apartment, Tiki would've reacted."

"Great point. Let's see what we can find outside." Boss led them out the door to the front of the building and then to Elena's SUV.

As the first light of dawn broke, they spotted a faint trail in the loose gravel, a telltale sign of something—or someone—being dragged. And Pup was willing to bet his last dollar it wasn't her suitcases.

They peered into the SUV, and their eyes landed on her suitcases, the only items inside. Frustration bubbled up. Dammit.

After they returned to the apartment, Pup found himself holding Elena's purse. A wave of curiosity washed over him. Should he take a peek inside, or would that be stepping over an invisible line? Suddenly, a new idea sparked in his mind.

"Sugar. Do you still have reliable contacts on the

SWAT teams?" Baltimore was home to three SWAT teams, and they hoped only Elena's former team was tainted, with the others remaining honest.

She nodded, her eyes widening with determination. "I do. I'm not sure how much they can help, but I can try." With that, she stepped away, phone in hand.

Boss glanced at his watch, a hint of urgency in his eyes. "Shoot, I've got to bolt. We're leaving for an op this morning."

Why wasn't Jesse halting everything with one of their agents missing?

As if sensing Pup's thoughts, Boss reassured him, "Don't worry. The brothers are here, along with some of Charlie team, if you need backup."

Backup? They were entrusting him with the mission to find Elena? It seemed almost surreal, but he was determined to lead the charge, ensuring no stone was left unturned in the search for her.

"Can you handle it?"

Though fear gnawed at him, he was resolute in his desire to lead this operation. "I can do that."

"Good. Sugar will stay. She's a fantastic liaison with the trustworthy members of the force." Boss paused, then turned back. "I hate leaving, but I trust you can manage. Good luck." With that, Boss kissed his wife, who was engrossed in a phone call, and then departed, leaving him once more questioning why all operations weren't called off.

Sure, there were six brothers, two former FBI agent wives, and countless members of Charlie team, but still….

Sugar ended the call. "The team has gone to ground, so we can assume they've got her."

Even though he already knew, the realization hit hard, twisting his gut with anxiety. "Okay." Then he remembered that he was in charge. What was his next move? Recalling the purse in his hands, he decided to open it. She could be furious all she wanted, but by all means, there could be something crucial here. What? He had no clue, but hope was his guiding light.

Sensing his reluctance to delve into Elena's private belongings, Sugar reached out. "Here, let me."

With a mix of hesitation and trust, he handed over the small black bag for her to examine.

As she settled on the couch to open it, a sudden commotion at the front door caught his attention. He stepped away, opening the door to welcome the entire Hamilton family—except for the kids. The wives, each bringing their unique skills, were ready to assist.

Jesse led the charge. "We're here. Let's get to work. Her phone is turned off. What have you got?"

But he had nothing, absolutely nothing. How could he possibly track down the woman who had captured his heart when he had no leads and no phone signal? Fear surged through him at the thought of losing her, just as he had finally found the one he wanted to spend forever with.

Chapter Twenty-Eight

Elena jolted awake, her heart pounding as she discovered herself bound to a chair, both arms and legs tightly secured with zip ties—not just one set but two on each limb. If only she had been more alert, she might have managed to leave some slack to break free, but now the ties dug into her skin, a painful reminder of her predicament. Panic surged through her as she took in her surroundings, realizing she was in a SWAT training house, far from the safety of the police grounds. Yet, she was sure Mark was the one who had incapacitated her. Why was she here?

Her hope dwindled as she realized her back pocket was empty. Her phone was gone. What would Pup think when he woke up alone, without a word from her? And what about Tiki? She was sure her dog would sense something was amiss and alert someone. She felt it deep in her bones.

Why had she kept the truth about her connection with SWAT from Jesse? It wasn't just the looming sexual harassment lawsuit that weighed on her. She had witnessed them accepting a bribe from the mayor, a secret they were determined to keep. The nature of the bribe remained a mystery to her, but she knew it was something sinister. They had even offered her a share, but she had turned it down, resolute in her decision to leave the team without tarnishing her reputation.

"Oh, so you're awake." Mark stepped into the bare, unsettling room. An empty chair faced hers, and he settled into it, leaving the room otherwise empty.

"Why, Mark?" She strained against her restraints, searching for any chance of escape.

"You know too much. There's no point. We've secured you with two zip ties."

"What is this all about?" She was bewildered by Mark's involvement in SWAT's corruption. It was a revelation that left her mind reeling.

"You know about the bribe."

Confused as to how he knew about it, and on edge, she decided to play dumb. "I don't know what you're talking about."

Suddenly, a familiar voice cut through the tension from the doorway. It was Paul, her old SWAT team leader, a man she despised. "Come, come." He stepped into the room. "You know all about the bribe we took from his father."

Elena's eyes snapped back to Mark, disbelief etched on her face. "The mayor is your father? I thought you said your father was dead." Why had he kept this secret from her for so long?

Mark sighed heavily, the weight of that revelation hanging in the air. "My stepfather is dead. But the mayor is my birth father. I don't like telling people since he's terrible at being a mayor. It's embarrassing."

The admission was overwhelming. For three long years, Mark had hidden this secret from her. What other truths lie buried? Her curiosity about the bribe soared like a bird set free. She fixed her gaze on Mark, her voice sharp with demand. "What was it for?"

"It's not important."

"Tell her, Mark. Tell her how you killed those people in that car, then drove away."

Mark's eyes fell, but Elena's anger flared brighter than the shock of her capture. "You murdered someone?"

Mark's head snapped up. "No. No. It was a car accident. It was an accident."

She strained against her restraints, her fury boiling over. "It's the same fucking thing."

Paul sneered. "Now, you know everything. The real question is what to do with you."

"I haven't told anyone, and I won't." She kept her voice steady despite the fear clawing at her insides. She knew her life was hanging by a thread, and she was willing to say anything to secure her freedom, even if it meant lying.

She cursed herself for not confiding in Jesse about the bribe. She had wanted to let it slide, to let them enjoy their little game while she prepared to roast them with a sexual harassment lawsuit. But now, with the truth about the bribe laid bare, she couldn't walk away. Lives had been lost, and Mark needed to face the consequences of his actions. His true parentage was irrelevant to her.

"Tsk, tsk. I don't believe you, Elena." Paul's voice

was laced with skepticism as he stood behind Mark.

"It's the truth. I don't want to get tangled up in this whole mess." But deep down, she knew justice was calling her name.

"We took a team vote. With the lawsuit—which is cute by the way—we've decided you're no longer valuable to this world." The words hung in the air, a chilling declaration that sent shivers down Elena's spine.

Mark leapt from his chair, his eyes blazing with defiance as he faced Paul. "You said you were only going to scare her, so you've scared her. Now, let her go."

Elena felt a wave of shock and gratitude as Mark stood up for her. Perhaps he was haunted by the thought of another life lost, but she didn't care. In this moment of peril, any ally was a blessing.

Paul's eyes narrowed. "I'm not sure we can trust her. And, you don't have a say in this. You're lucky we're keeping our word."

Mark spun back to Elena, desperation in his voice. "They blackmailed me to get you. I swear."

Before Elena could process his words, Paul delivered a brutal sucker punch, sending Mark crashing to the cold concrete floor, blood trickling from his head. The room fell silent, the tension palpable as the gravity of the situation sank in.

This was it. She was about to face her end for a senseless reason, not for the noble cause of saving someone, as she had always dreamed. That's why she had joined the police force, then advanced to SWAT. But after a disillusioning experience, she sought refuge at HIS, a place where she could help those in need without the taint of corruption.

She hadn't even had the chance to truly embrace her feelings for Pup. She was relieved she hadn't confessed her love, even though it had nearly escaped her lips during their intimate moments. She couldn't bear the thought of that being his final memory of her. She wished for him to remember her in his arms, not as someone mourning a love lost.

"So, what are you waiting for?" Her voice was steady and defiant, ready to face whatever lay ahead.

Paul glanced up at Mark, his eyes narrowed. "The rest of the team. They want everyone here to witness the consequences of betraying us."

"But I didn't betray you!" Her shout echoed in the room. "I let it go."

Paul shot her a look of pure disdain before striding out of the room, leaving her alone with the unconscious Mark. He paused at the door, his voice dripping with menace. "I'll be back to take care of him."

Her mind raced with uncertainty about his intentions, but she couldn't let Mark be tied up. If he awoke, he might leave and alert HIS, potentially securing her freedom.

"Mark." She glanced nervously at the door to ensure Paul was out of earshot. "Mark, wake up."

He remained motionless, but she clung to hope, refusing to consider escape. Her chair, a cold metal contraption, offered no solace. She had mastered the art of breaking wooden chairs, at least enough to free her body, if not her limbs. But this time, they had anticipated her every move.

"Oh, Pup. Tiki knows this place."

If only they could get her near, she'd go ballistic with her eagerness to manage the house in a practiced takedown. Only this time, it wouldn't be practice.

Sighing, she waited until Mark woke or Paul and the team returned. One offering an opportunity to escape. The other signally her demise.

"Come on, HIS. Be the company I think you are. Find me."

****

Pup was in a bind, with no clues about her whereabouts. They had been correct about the SWAT team's involvement, but the question remained of where they had taken her. The clock was ticking, and he was determined to find her.

Devon's words broke into his lost thoughts. "If her phone is turned back on, we'll have her location."

"If" was the elusive word.

Pup was taken aback when he glanced at the door and saw Daylan and Buddy standing there. What were they doing here? He hadn't summoned them. Daylan was one of the last people he wanted to encounter.

As he navigated through Elena's apartment, now transformed into a makeshift headquarters, he halted in front of the man at the doorway. "What are you doing here?"

Daylan raised his hands defensively. "Look. I'm sorry, but that doesn't matter. I figured if we find an area to search, three dogs are better than two."

Pup had to admit that Daylan made a valid point. He

could use all the assistance he could muster. "Would you take the dogs out for a bit? They need to walk." He knew it was a task he should handle himself, but he couldn't bear to leave her apartment. Of everyone here, Daylan was the best suited to manage the dogs.

Daylan nodded. "I can do that."

Pup called the K9s, and they eagerly dashed out the door after Daylan and Buddy. One problem solved, he thought, but the real challenge lay ahead. He approached Sugar, who was sitting beside Devon on the couch.

"Sugar, where do you think they'd take her?"

She bit her lip, a sigh escaping her lips. "I hate to say this, but it depends on what they plan to do with her."

The words hit him like a punch to the gut. What horrors were they inflicting on her? Had they already ended her life and were now disposing of her body? The thought was unbearable.

"Okay, let's hope they're only holding her somewhere." His heart clung to hope that it was that, instead of a worst-case scenario.

"Well, they might take her to one of the outbuildings where we practice away from police grounds."

It was a lead, at least. Before he could fire off another question, Devon suddenly sat up straighter. "How many?"

Sugar bit her lip once more. "Let me see. I remember three, but I'm not sure if there are any new ones. I'll check." She stood up, phone to her ear, and hurried away.

"What do you think?" Pup's eyes filled with anticipation. "Can you track them down?"

Devon nodded confidently. "It'll be quicker if Sugar hands over the addresses, but I'm up for the challenge. What's your plan?"

Here they were, looking to him for guidance. It was almost surreal that one of the Hamilton brothers was asking for his input. Their trust in him was a powerful boost to his self-assurance.

"It's a start. It's better than just sitting around with no leads." Then a thought struck him. "What about her ex? Have you looked into him?"

Devon nodded. "He's clean. Except for the arrest, he's only had a few traffic tickets."

Pup wasn't convinced. The ex being out there after they suspected him of vandalizing her apartment was unsettling. He might not be SWAT material, but wealthy individuals could easily hire someone to do their dirty work.

"I think we need to find him. I can't explain it, but something tells me he's involved."

"You need to chat with your landlord about those outside cameras not working. It would've been a breeze if we could've caught the action."

Pup let out a grunt. It was probably around three in the morning, and even if the cameras were functioning, the darkness would've made it hard to see much.

Sugar came back with news. "One of the teams is already at a house practicing, so only two are left empty."

With a plan in mind, he turned as Daylan returned with the dogs. "I'll take Tiki and Casey to one house, and Daylan can take Buddy to the other."

Jesse approached. "That sounds like a solid plan.

We'll split up with you."

Having the Hamilton family on his side lifted his spirits, giving him hope that they'd find her. But he had to keep in mind that they weren't sure she was there. This was a long shot. But he was willing to take it.

Chapter Twenty-Nine

With Jesse behind the wheel, Pup set off from Elena's apartment, accompanied by Brad, Jake, and the two dogs. The pups were nestled in the back of Jesse's SUV, with Tiki whimpering for her beloved owner. Speaking of ownership, Pup decided it was time to address something that had been weighing on him.

"Jesse, I'd like to adopt Casey. Would you be willing to sell her?" He was ready to spend every penny of his life savings to make Casey his own, as he couldn't bear the thought of her returning to the kennels.

Jesse shot him a quick glance before refocusing on the road. "No, we won't sell her."

Pup's heart sank, but he nodded, accepting the answer. "Okay."

Then, with a surprising twist, Jesse smiled. "Pup, we've already decided to gift you Casey as your own. We've decided that HIS won't own any dogs because we prefer the dogs with their handlers all the time."

Pup's heart soared. They were giving him Casey. Just like that? Overwhelmed with joy, he quickly composed himself, not wanting to risk their decision. "Thank you. That's very generous of you." He struggled to find the right words, knowing he should leave it at that.

"You're welcome. We can discuss this later, but know that she's yours."

Casey was his. All his. He closed his eyes, savoring the happiness, though he knew he had to set it aside for now.

The mission was clear. Find Elena. Jesse's phone buzzed, and he answered through the Bluetooth speaker. Devon's voice crackled through, delivering the most thrilling news. "Her phone was on for a few minutes. If she hasn't moved, she's at your destination. I've rerouted the other team."

A wave of relief washed over Pup. He had no idea how her phone had turned on, but he was grateful for the lead. Plus, they were already halfway there.

"What's the plan once we get there?"

It was unusual for the big boss, who typically orchestrated operations, to seek Pup's guidance. Fortunately, Sugar had provided them with brief sketches of the buildings to search. Pup knew Tiki would lead them to Elena, as she was intimately familiar with the building.

"We park down the block and observe the building." Pup's heart pounded with the urge to rush in and save her. "Once we assess the situation, we act. Tiki will lead since she's not only familiar with the building but can also pick up Elena's scent."

Jesse nodded approvingly. "Solid plan."

That nod of approval lifted Pup's spirits. Although

the plan seemed easy and straightforward, the validation gave him renewed hope for its success.

As they pulled onto the side street near the practice facility, Pup's frustration simmered beneath the surface. Three vehicles were parked there, and Devon reported that one belonged to Elena's ex. Pup couldn't shake the feeling that this man was somehow entangled in the situation. Another was owned by Elena's former team leader, Paul Griffin. The final one belonged to someone Sugar said was new to the team, taking Elena's spot—Robert Haines.

Pup's mind raced with questions. Would the rest of the team show up, or were they already inside? The uncertainty gnawed at him, a persistent itch he couldn't ignore. Despite his urge to take action, Pup decided to wait for the rest of the team, in case they encountered a whole SWAT team well-versed in the building's layout.

"That's a wise decision." Jesse offered a reassuring nod that strengthened Pup's resolve.

"It's tearing me apart." His gaze remained fixed on the looming building.

"You really have feelings for her, don't you?"

Pup glanced at the backseat, but Brad and Jake were engrossed in the building plans on a tablet. He turned back, letting out a heavy sigh. Meeting his boss's eyes, he confessed, "I love her. I know it's soon, and everyone might think I'm too young to understand, but I do. I love her. I'm not sure if she feels the same, but I need to find out."

Jesse observed him thoughtfully before nodding. "We'll get her out. And, Pup, when you know, you know."

The tension in the air was palpable as they sat in silence, Pup's patience fraying at the edges. If the second team hadn't arrived just in the nick of time, he would have charged in alone—him and Tiki, consequences be damned. His resolve was unshakable. He was determined to rescue her.

Pup looked around at the group. "Suit up."

The team sprang into action, donning bulletproof vests over their T-shirts, ready for whatever lay ahead.

Pup meticulously checked his gun in its leg holster before summoning Daylan. He met the man's gaze with a steely determination. "Look, I know this is a shit job, but I need you to stay with Casey and Buddy. They don't need to be in there."

Daylan's jaw clenched, but he nodded, acknowledging the gravity of the situation. "You're right. Are you sure about taking Tiki? With only three legs…."

Pup knew what Daylan wasn't saying. Tiki was limited in attack mode, but Pup had faith that with her owner being held captive, the dog would rise to the challenge. "She'll do fine."

"Do you want me to harness her?"

Pup appreciated the thoughtfulness. "That'd be great. The bulletproof vest is on the floorboard."

One of the things Pup cherished about HIS was their commitment to their K9s, providing them with bulletproof vests—a luxury many police forces struggled to afford.

With a deep breath, Pup gave Tiki her first command, "Fuss," ensuring she stayed close as they approached the building. He couldn't afford any surprises. Sneaking around to the back, where a lone window was their only entry, Pup and Tiki led the charge to the front of the building, leaving Kate and Rylee to guard the window.

Pup's heart pounded in his chest. The weight of the decision to breach the building was almost unbearable. One misstep could have dire consequences. Yet, Tiki's whine beside him was a reassuring presence. Inspired by her, Pup resolved to follow her lead. Together, they could pull off this daring rescue of Elena, minimizing any bloodshed.

Pup's heart pounded as he tested the doorknob, hoping it would turn. Cowboy was unavailable to blow the door, and the thought of waiting for a ram was unbearable. To his relief, the knob clicked open, and a wave of tension washed over him.

He quickly scanned the team, ensuring everyone was ready for the mission ahead. With adrenaline coursing through his veins, he disconnected Tiki's leash and barked the building search command to her, "Tiki, voran revier," and then shouted into his open mic, "Go. Go. Go."

The team surged forward, he and Tiki leading the charge. The knowledge that their opponents were armed with live rounds kept Pup on high alert, staying close to Tiki. Despite her protective vest, her past injury—a lost leg—served as a grim reminder of the dangers they faced.

As the teams meticulously combed through each room, Pup and Tiki embarked on a mission to find Elena. Tiki was relentless, her paws pattering down one hallway and into another until she abruptly halted before a door, sitting down and gazing up at Pup with a whine.

"In here, huh?" He tested the knob. It turned easily. He surmised they hadn't anticipated her new teammates would rescue her. Or, it was a trap. Well, her SWAT buddies weren't expecting the HIS team.

Behind him, Jesse and Jake stood poised, ready for action. With a silent three-finger countdown, on the count of one, Pup pushed the door open, taking in the tense scene before him.

Elena sat in the center of the room, bound to a chair. Another man was also tied to a chair, but his back was turned to Pup, obscuring his identity. Pup knew he wasn't a threat—yet.

Tiki, a testament to her training, awaited the next command but growled and remained fixated on the man with a gun to Elena's head.

He stood behind her, concealing his body from view, clearly wearing a bulletproof vest just like them.

In his earpiece, Daylan's voice crackled. "You've got company. Looks like the rest of the team has arrived. Three new tangos."

Dammit. This mission would've been a breeze if they hadn't shown up.

"We've got it covered," AJ reassured over the comms, a lifeline of hope.

A wave of relief washed over Pup. Now, the real challenge was how to get Elena out without this man pulling the trigger.

Pup eyed the man whose steady hand held the gun to his woman's head. "You know there's no way out, Paul."

Devon had sent a chilling image of Elena's former team leader, who now stood menacingly before them.

"Oh, I'm fine sacrificing my life for this bitch." Paul's words were a dagger.

That wasn't the response Pup had anticipated, and he found himself at a loss. How do you reason with a man who has nothing to lose? The tension was palpable, and the gun could go off at any moment.

"And don't send that dog over here, or I'll shoot the bitch."

Pup had no intention of sending the K9 over just yet. His priority was to disarm Paul and free Elena from the gun's deadly grip.

His eyes were glued to Paul, daring not to meet Elena's gaze, fearing it would spell disaster. The sight of her bound tore at his heart, and he vowed this man would face the consequences.

"Everyone has something to lose."

"If she lives, she ruins my life. I won't go to prison."

So, this was a murder-suicide. Fuck. Fuck. Fuck. Pup glanced at Jesse for support, and his boss nodded to him, giving him courage.

"Tell me, Paul, were you also her stalker?" The idea had come to him when they were analyzing the first suspects. The stalker had vanished when the issues started.

"Of course. Who else would stalk this bitch? Not Loverboy over there." With his head, Paul gestured to the man in the chair.

Pup didn't look back. He knew who he'd find. "Mark, fucking, Thompson." He wondered how he'd ended up tied up, then brushed off the thought. He had to stay focused, but if Paul called her a bitch one more time, he was sending in Tiki.

Pup observed Paul's hand begin to tremble. Thankfully, his finger wasn't on the trigger, a testament to his training as a SWAT officer. Paul was all talk, no action. A flicker of hope ignited within him as he glanced down at Elena.

In that moment, their eyes locked. Her eyes were filled with anguish, yet there flickered steely determination. She subtly shook her head.

She didn't want action. No way. He would rescue her. Perhaps she was hinting at avoiding Tiki. He knew how much she adored that dog and how she'd be devastated if anything happened to her. Her eyes darted down, then quickly snapped back up, leaving him guessing.

That's when he realized she had a plan. But what could she possibly do? She was tied to a chair.

He scrunched up his brow, trying to decipher her meaning. Then it hit him—she'd do the only thing she could do.

And with a graceful move, she acted. Strapped to a chair, Elena managed to stand partially, leaning forward, the chair legs kicking back, sending Paul stumbling backward. She shouted, "Tiki, fass!" before Paul steadied himself.

Tiki broke free from Pup's side as she ran past Elena, charging at Paul, who raised his arms to block. Tiki jumped, and her teeth bit into the arm holding the gun.

Paul's yowl of pain echoed through the room. Jesse and Jake quickly moved in, covering Paul and removing his weapon, while Pup focused on the man in the other chair.

His eyes locked onto the man with dried blood

smeared across his face, a man who seemed to radiate anger. "Friend or foe?"

"Neither." Elena's voice was steady, yet filled with disgust.

"We've got the three at the front subdued," AJ reported through the comms, breaking the tension slightly.

Only then did he reach into his pocket, retrieving a knife to free Elena.

"Stop!" Elena's voice pierced the still air. "There's one more unless you've caught him."

Pup's instincts kicked in, and he spun towards the door, snagging his gun from the leg holster and at the ready. Seeing Elena was safe, he had momentarily forgotten about the third car and the mysterious new team member lurking inside.

Adrenaline surged through him, but fear ate away at his insides. He'd messed up. Big time.

There, at the threshold, stood a man in a SWAT uniform, hands raised in surrender. "I'm not fighting you. I want none of this." He spat on the ground with disdain. "They're a bunch of criminals."

Pup's gaze hardened as he locked eyes with Robert Haines. "Are you armed?" He didn't have any visible weapons, but that didn't mean anything with a SWAT member.

Robert shook his head. "Disarmed in the next room."

Smart man. Over comms, Pup called, "I need two for the final tango." Then a thought occurred, and he cocked his head. "Are you the one who turned on her phone?"

Robert nodded, a mix of defiance and resignation in his expression. "I couldn't stand by for this, and it was all I could think to do since I couldn't overpower Paul here."

Brad and Kate arrived to take care of Robert. As he was being escorted out, he shot a pointed glance at Paul. "Are you going to let that dog go or what?"

Pup stiffened. Sure enough, Elena had forgotten to give Tiki the release command, and the dog clung stubbornly to Paul's arm.

Amidst Paul's screams, Elena's voice barely cut through. "Aus!" She then turned to Pup with a sheepish grin. "Oops."

Pup couldn't stifle his chuckle. He adored this woman.

He turned his knife on her restraints. With each cut, he murmured apologies, acutely aware of the pain he was causing.

"Why didn't you think of that earlier?" He deftly cut a zip tie around her ankle.

"Because I'd still be stuck in this cursed chair, and he'd have just pulled the trigger."

"That gun could've gone off at any moment." His heart was pounding at the close call. This seemingly straightforward rescue mission had nearly spiraled out of control, and he would have lost the woman who meant the most to him.

Thankfully, Tiki had saved the day. That dog had earned her hero status once again.

When Elena was finally free, he ignored the dog whining at their feet, and Pup pulled her into his arms, holding her tightly as if he was afraid she might disappear.

"Elena, don't ever scare me like that again." With a

fierce determination, he kissed her passionately, oblivious to the Hamilton brothers watching. He loved her, and he was determined to show it.

Finally pulling back and separating them a few steps, he began, "I—"

"How disgustingly sweet. So, you just jump from me to this…kid."

Pup's back stiffened, and his anger flared. He'd never punched a bound man, but this man was asking for it. "Mark Thompson, I'd say it's a pleasure to meet you, but it's not. You can stay tied up until the cops get here." He didn't care if Mark was innocent. At least he wasn't a physical threat, just a verbal one.

In a moment of sheer audacity, Mark hurled a racial slur at Elena.

Before Pup could even think about landing a punch, Elena struck with lightning speed, sending Mark's head snapping sideways with a powerful jab to the jaw.

She retracted her hand, muttering something in Spanish. "I forgot how much that hurts."

Pup raised an eyebrow, intrigued. "Was it worth it?"

Elena grinned, her eyes sparkling with satisfaction. "Yes, it was very satisfying."

She knelt and petted Tiki, praising her while Rylee arrived to guard Mark.

Then, with a swift motion, Elena stood and dashed to him, enveloping him in a passionate embrace and kissing him as if her life depended on it. He held onto her, hoping with all his heart that this was just the beginning of their eternal journey together.

Chapter Thirty

After a marathon of explaining everything to the police chief, Elena and Jesse were finally free, albeit with a stern reminder to reach out to the police first in the future. Elena couldn't help but think that if faced with a similar situation, they might do the same thing.

Now, she had a daunting task ahead of sitting down with Pup to lay it all out and apologize for not trusting him enough to share everything sooner. Their whirlwind of back-and-forth, passionate encounters and the harrowing kidnapping had left little room for clarity. When had there ever been a moment to pause?

She scolded herself silently. There had been ample time to share everything with him. Trusting him had been a quick journey, and she should have taken it.

As Jesse pulled up to her apartment building, she expressed her gratitude.

"Are you going to be okay?" Jesse's face was a canvas of concern.

She would be. Sure, she might feel a bit on edge for a while, but she knew she could weather this storm. With a nod, she opened the SUV door. "I'll be fine. Thanks again."

He chuckled. "You really need to stop thanking me. That's about the hundredth time. This is what we do for family."

In her experience, most families didn't carry guns and track down villains to save you. They usually relied on the police. But when HIS knew they couldn't, they took action. She couldn't be more grateful. "Gotcha."

As Jesse left, Elena hesitated by her SUV, contemplating whether to grab her luggage. But the urgency of the moment pushed her forward.

The police chief had dismissed the teams, leaving only her and Jesse to endure his stern lecture and heartfelt gratitude. Pup had been reluctant to go, but Jesse had insisted. The sight of his dejected face as she said goodbye was one she wouldn't soon forget.

As she reached for her keys to unlock the front door of her apartment building, the door unexpectedly buzzed open. Confused, she glanced around, wondering who else was being buzzed in, but decided to step inside.

There, in his open doorway, stood Pup. He moved towards her with a determined look and enveloped her in a hug so tight that she had to chuckle and ask him to ease up so she could catch her breath.

"Sorry." He finally released his grip, but not his hold. "Thank God, you're safe." He pulled back, his lips meeting hers with an intensity that sent electric shivers through her body. She was in love with this man and was determined to tell him, no matter how unprepared he might be. She sensed he felt something for her, too. Why else would he go to such lengths to guide Tiki—and not Casey—to her rescue? Tiki was relentless, always finding her way.

As if on cue, the dogs burst out of Pup's apartment, bounding around their legs with wagging tails. Elena broke the kiss, laughter bubbling up as she knelt to hug Tiki and pet Casey. "Tiki, my girl, you're a hero once again."

Tiki responded with a joyful lick to her face, making Elena giggle even more. She looked up at Pup. "Thank you for using Tiki. She despised that man as much as I did."

With a mischievous glint in his eye, Pup chuckled. "I'd say she did, judging by the way she bit him."

As they straightened up, they rounded up the dogs and made their way to Pup's apartment. He took her hand in his, his eyes filled with curiosity. "So, are you finally going to spill the beans on what this whole thing was really about?"

She nodded, her voice steady as she revealed everything. She spoke of her tumultuous relationship with Mark, the intense involvement with the SWAT team, the harrowing sexual harassment lawsuit, and the shocking bribe. Then, she recounted the jaw-dropping revelation of Mark's true identity and how he had been ensnared in a web of blackmail himself.

Pup let out a whistle, his eyes wide with disbelief. "Wow. They say when I do it, I do it big. But you, my Elena, you do it bigger."

Her heart swelled at the sound of him calling her "His Elena." Yet, there was still much to discuss before they could delve into the depths of their feelings.

Or was there? No, they had already said enough.

"Kevin." She watched his eyes widen in surprise at the use of his real name.

He straightened up, his posture tense. "This must be serious if you're calling me Kevin."

It was indeed the most serious conversation she had ever faced. She nodded, her heart pounding. "It is. I have been horrible to you."

He gently played with her fingers, a hint of a smile on his lips. "That's water under the bridge."

She was grateful for his forgiveness. She had never intended to be unkind, but it had happened, and an apology was long overdue. She took a deep breath, steeling herself for the difficult part. "I'm done."

His hand froze in hers, and the wave of despair that washed over him nearly broke her heart.

"I'm done putting up roadblocks. I know I'm much older than you—"

As he tried to interrupt, she squeezed his hand firmly. "Let me finish."

Pup nodded and squeezed her hand back in silent support.

"Age and being your boss are just excuses. I'd walk away from Lead Handler in a heartbeat to be with you."

He moved closer, his eyes intense. "You can't leave the job. You're amazing at it."

She laughed softly. "That's what catches your attention? Not the part where I'm confessing my love for you?"

Before she could say more, he captured her lips in a

fierce kiss that left her breathless when he finally pulled away.

"Thank goodness. Because, woman, I love you too, and I was sick of hearing those flimsy excuses for why we couldn't be together."

He pulled her into his arms, holding her close as the couch's awkwardness forced him to shift, eventually lying her down beneath him.

"Not yet." Her heart was racing with desire and a need for clarity. "We need to talk about what we're going to do."

Pup grinned, his eyes sparkling with hope. "That's easy. You move in here and we live happily-ever-after."

"No, Pup. I just spent the last three years living with someone. I need my space."

He sat back, and she followed suit, the weight of their conversation settling between them.

"Well, you've got a year on your lease, so how about I give you that time and then you move in here. Or, I can move in there. It doesn't matter."

The thought of finding a house together next year crossed her mind, but she kept it to herself, knowing it was too soon to leap into such a future.

"But you should spend your nights here. Every night. Can we agree on that?"

Elena's heart fluttered at the thought, but she hesitated. She tilted her head, considering. "Most nights?"

"All nights."

With a nod and a smile, Elena agreed. "All nights."

She knew deep down that by the end of the year, she'd be living with him. He'd offer her the space she craved, but for now, she needed to stand on her own. If only to prove to herself that she could thrive without relying on a man, even if he were the love of her life.

"What do you think Jesse will say?"

He gently guided her back down on the couch, settling on top of her. "Who cares?" His breath was warm against her neck as he kissed it.

"It will matter if he decides we can't be together and work together."

"It's okay. As long as we don't bring our fights to work."

"Fights?"

"Yes." He kissed her nose. "We will fight, of course. There's no hope for it with your fiery temper."

She playfully swatted at him. "My fiery temper? How about your stubbornness?"

He feigned injury. "Okay, we agree that we will disagree, but we won't bring it to work."

"Agreed. Now, kiss me."

And he did, their tongues meeting like old friends, tangling and dueling for dominance, igniting a fiery spark that coursed through her.

The dogs whined, interrupting the tender kiss, and Pup broke away with a playful curse. He settled back. "I was planning to take them out before you showed up. Care to join me for a walk?"

Her heart swelled with warmth at his care for Tiki, as if she were his own. "Sure." As she sat, she tucked her braid back and smoothed her dressy shirt, wishing she'd changed before meeting him, having been dressed for Aaron.

"Oh my gosh!" She'd nearly forgotten. "They caught Zee's bomber. Can you imagine it was one of her twin advisors? They've been inseparable since high school."

"Wow." He grabbed the leashes from the wall and handed one to her. "I always had a hunch something was off about that three-way relationship."

"Absolutely." She attached the leash to Tiki. "Ready to go, girl?"

Tiki barked joyfully, her tail wagging furiously.

"I have news of my own." He clipped the leash on Casey. "Jesse gave me Casey."

A wave of excitement surged through her, and she embraced him. "That's incredible."

He returned the hug. "It's truly amazing. I don't know what I would've done without this girl."

"Family." Her voice was filled with emotion.

"Family."

Their bond strengthened with each word.

"I love you, Kevin."

"I love you, Elena." Then he grinned. "Did you know that dogs…."

ABOUT THE AUTHOR

Sheila Kell writes about romantic men who leave women's hearts pounding with a happily ever after built on memorable, adrenaline-pumping stories. She is a four-time winner of the Readers' Favorite Book Award for romantic suspense and contemporary romance.

As a Southern girl who has left behind her days with the United States Air Force and as a University Vice President, she can usually be found in central Florida with her family and cats. When she isn't writing, you can find Sheila with her nose in a good book, trying to leash train her cats, or wishing she had a genie to do her bidding.

Ways to connect
https://www.sheilakellbooks.com
https://www.facebook.com/sheilakellbooks
https://www.goodreads.com/sheilakellbooks
https://www.bookbub.com/authors/sheila-kell
Sheila loves to hear directly from readers. Feel free to email her at sheila@sheilakell.com.

Don't miss out on new releases, exclusive excerpts, and giveaways! Join her newsletter:
https://www.SheilaKell.com/subscribe